My Name is Karma

An Amazing Tale

Based on True Life Experiences

CANDY C KNIGHT

ISBN: 1978149034
ISBN-13: 978-1978149038

DEDICATION

To every Karma in the world:

Stay strong!
Don't let bullies and backstabbers keep you down.
They'll learn someday — it's not nice to mess with Karma!

***

To everyone who encouraged me to keep going
when I felt like giving up, my inner Karma thanks you!

Enjoy the story!

ACKNOWLEDGMENTS

Extra special thank you to the following:

Franz Chenet
Thank you for your graphic artistry and
willingness to help a friend fulfill her dreams.

Marilyn Wiest
Thank you for listening to my endless rants.

**April Lapetoda, Jodi Ames, Laura DeLeon,
Lacie Carmody and Kathryn Barnsley**
Thanks for being my "readers" and
telling me the truth about Karma

To everyone whose names I'm forgetting at the moment
Don't worry, I'll get you in the next book

Finally ...

To Mama
Thank you most of all for yelling at me
to get back to work and finish this book!
Love you!

PROLOGUE
IT'S A WONDERFUL LIFE!

"Randy, have Graphics finished the layout for the Christmas spread?" I asked my secretary.

"No, Ms. Bailey," Randy answered. "They said they need until tomorrow evening to finish."

I ensured my voice was calm yet stern when I replied. "Go down there and make it clear they'll have that spread ready by three today, or they'll have all day tomorrow to look for new jobs."

Randy nodded. She stood at attention, about three feet in front of my desk — notepad and pen in hand and ready to jot down my next command. She always stood this way, and always three feet in front of my desk — no more, no less.

Maybe I shouldn't have told her that her glasses, and her breath, reminded me of my dead grandmother.

It took me a while, but one day I noticed she'd gotten new and more fashionable frames. She also always had a mint or some type of sweet in her mouth. She kept a can of breath mints in her middle desk drawer, which I noticed she regularly replenished every week.

I didn't bother to look up from my reports. "Well?"

"Yes, ma'am?"

"Why are you still here? *Get your butt down to graphics!*"

"Yes, ma'am!" She did a quick about-face and high-tailed it

out of my office. She ran off so quickly, she hadn't noticed Kevin, my executive IT technician, coming toward her.

They smashed into each other, and Kevin dropped the tablet and the papers he carried. He mumbled a few expletives at her, but either Randy didn't hear him or she hadn't cared, because she didn't stop to apologize.

Oh no, when the boss said run — Randy ran.

That girl. She wasn't the brightest bulb, but she was the best assistant I'd ever had. With a little more seasoning and the right bit of toughness, she just might make a good manager someday.

At thirty-five-years old, I was one of the few women in the world to be president and CEO of my own multi-million pound, international company — Karma Marketing Services. Not only an Oxford graduate, I was also the mum of two rumbustious boys and the sweetest baby girl on the planet, as well as a recent recipient of London's Humanitarian of the Year award.

Since six-thirty in the morning, I'd been sitting at my desk, reviewing employee appraisals, new project bids, emails for major clients, and all the other crap a CEO must deal with every day. The clock ticked another second off the day, and I wondered if I'd ever get today's work done.

"I see your assistant is off to decree another of her majesty's commands, Karma," came a deep voice from the office doorway.

I looked up to see Eric, my CFO, leaning against my door. This six-foot Adonis — with his sexy Scottish accent — looked so darn good in his dark Armani suit, £600 tie and £2,000 watch. He stepped in and closed the door.

Eric had a body that made women giddy and men jealous. When he entered a room you just had to stop what you were doing and simply revel in his amazing features. His face was perfectly symmetrical, strong and defined. His eyes were a mesmerizing dusty brown with just a hint of hazel green.

A prominent jaw curved gracefully around the strength of his neck and snaking cords of muscle shaped his entire body; strong arms, muscular thighs and calves, a powerful chest and abdomen, and a firm butt added to the package.

But it was his lips that took top prize. Yes, those beautiful, round, sultry, succulent lips.

Aww, those lips, and what I imagined them doing to mine, made me weak in the knees every time I caught a glimpse of this handsome descendant of the Roman gods.

I stole a glance at his butt when he bent over to pick up the latest copy of Rolling Stone magazine, and I nearly swooned as he flipped through the magazine and swayed his hips while humming the latest pop tune.

Handsome, dapper, smooth, majestic, clever, cunning, intelligent. These descriptions didn't do this man enough justice.

Yes, I know admiring a co-worker's looks in today's *"everyone gets a ribbon," "you can't say that," "this is my safe-space," "everyone's offended,"* corporate world is passé and can lead to multi-million pound lawsuits.

But c'mon! Is it harassment when the sexy god is your husband?

"Hi, love. How's your day going?" I asked.

"Not bad, but I could do with a little lunch," he replied.

"Sure, where do you want to —"

My breath caught as Eric gently pushed me back into my chair. The usually playful smile he normally greeted me with was replaced with a more devilish, yet sexy grin. And his perfect lips were ripe for kissing.

Oh and kiss me, they did. Oh my goodness! Why did his kisses always set my insides aflame? This man knew how to use his talented tongue — in the boardroom, the bedroom, and now the boss's office. Lord have mercy! His tongue actually tasted like chocolate and strawberries.

Eric's hypnotizing eyes stared deeply into mine. He slowly lifted me out of the chair and onto my desk and gently pressed his hard manhood against me. My back arched in anticipation as his anaconda teased my sweet spot.

Oh yeah, he's most certainly a descendant of the Roman gods.

Eric leaned over and flattened me onto the desk. He whispered my name as he thrust inside me.

"Karma, *Karma....*"

CHAPTER 1
"WHY ME?"

"KARMA!"

My head snapped up and I straighten my glasses. "Sorry Monica. What did you say?"

Monica Sander bent over my desk to whisper in my ear, yet she somehow still managed to ensure all the men in the department could see her large bum.

"I said get your head out of your arse," she whispered, "and hand me the sales reports for the Richmond's Sweets account I graciously allowed you to put together for me."

Monica worked in the client services department of Vixen Public Relations and Marketing. She and I both started at the company as research assistances about four years ago. When we first met, she was nice, sweet and posh. I thought we were gonna be good friends. I soon learned Monica's price for friendship was very expensive.

It didn't take long either — two weeks in fact — before Monica showed she'd do anything to move up in the company — including taking credit for work I had done on a project as part of my entry-level management training program application.

Thanks in part to my uncontrollable need to be liked, I didn't speak up then — nor any of the other times I did Monica's work for her. As a result, in the past four years Monica moved up the ladder and was now a leading client services associate. She'd also been recently named Employee of the Month. In those same four years, not only had I not received so much as a pay increase or sniffed a promotion, I'd been demoted to receptionist and secretary.

I know this sounds like jealously rearing its ugly head, but truth be told, I wasn't jealous. Not one iota. Monica worked harder for it — much, much harder.

Well, that is if you considered sleeping with every client who walked through door working harder for it. She took the company's mission of "servicing the client's every need" to heart. She was the very definition of the office slut who had slept her way to the top.

Yet, despite her willingness to bend over for the company, even she was surprised when she was passed over — for the fourth straight time — for a promotion to division manager.

Right now, I wish she had popped a breath mint in mouth before she spoke to me, if for no other reason than to mask the lingering stench of her latest dalliance.

"Of course Monica," I said and searched through the pile of papers on my desk for the reports I'd finished late last night.

"Hurry up? Jessica is coming and she needs those reports," Monica commanded.

I found the reports and handed them to her a split second before Jessica Paterson approached.

"Monica, where are those reports?" Jessica asked. "You said they'd be ready for the ten a.m. meeting."

"Here they are, Ms. Paterson." Monica handed the reports to her. Monica's fake sweet and polite tone irked me to no end.

Jessica Paterson — founder, president and CEO of Vixen PR and Marketing — skimmed over the pages. Known as "Florence Nightingale" in the public relations world, Jessica started Vixen ten years ago, after leaving her former employer and taking that company's top client with her. In those ten years she turned a small company with ten workers into a formidable corporation with over 250 employees handling more than £1 billion in accounts.

The company's success attracted a string of international corporations who begged, and handsomely paid, for Jessica's expertise and ability to enhance their reputations and brand. More importantly, companies hired Vixen to increase sales and profits.

Jessica Paterson. Her name was synonymous with successful women who didn't just break through the glass ceiling, but used that glass to slit the throats of her competition. She was a ruthless and manipulating bitch who demanded, and expected, loyalty, respect and professionalism from her employees.

And goshdarnit — I was jealous I couldn't be more like her.

Jessica wasn't the typical CEO. She hardly ever hid behind that huge oak desk in her top floor office. She didn't show up on certain days, issue orders and then jet off for expensive shopping sprees using company profits.

No, Jessica hardly spent any time in her office. At any given moment of the day her employees found her walking the halls in her stilettos, a mobile phone in one hand and some strange juice concoction in the other. She'd recently given up her daily café latte after the company landed the £45 million Juiced-Up account.

When she wasn't bulldozing her way through the building, she was out and about in the city — a snake charmer charming the clothes off everyone she met. She was always at some meeting, social event, or anywhere the bold, the beautiful and the filthy rich congregated. She always seemed to show up just in time with a pitch on how Vixen would increase their business's brand and profit, or how Vixen can help smooth over a damaging scandal.

Most importantly, she'd eloquently explained how Vixen's help translated into more money for the client.

Whatever she said or did worked because she enchanted clients so well they shelled out millions on the spot. Jessica's success made her the envy of other public relations firms, especially at her former employer, Carter Marketing and Public Relations. Jessica and Carter's current CEO hated each other.

Whenever an account was up for grabs, it was madness within both companies. The dirty tricks and attempts to discredit each other reminded me of that cartoon Spy vs. Spy — each company would do whatever was necessary to thwart the other and win the account. For the last three years, Vixen had won every round.

"Excuse me, Ms. Paterson, you have ten minutes before your nine o'clock with Frederickson's," Peter informed Jessica. She ignored him. I tried to hide my chuckle but he caught me, and stared daggers at me.

Peter Franks was Jessica's executive assistant — her very gay and extremely patronizing — executive assistant. I had only interacted with Peter once or twice since I've worked here.

And each time I wanted to toss him back in the closet and throw away the key.

"These are good. Nice job," Jessica said as she skimmed over the reports.

"Thank you," Monica and I said at the same time.

Jessica looked at me puzzled. Monica glared at me. Peter rolled his eyes. I shucked down into my chair and pretended to do some work on my computer.

"Peter, head back to my office," Jessica commanded. "I left the latest marketing portfolio on Crystal Rock Foods on my desk and I want to review them before lunch."

"Right away, Ms. Paterson," Peter replied and disappeared toward the lift. Monica rolled her eyes as Peter walked away. She and Peter didn't quite like each other much. Actually they detested each other.

About this time last year when it became known Jessica was looking for a new executive assistant, over seventy company employees, including me, applied. To be Jessica's executive assistant was as cushy a job a person would ever find. The position came with a lot a lucrative perks. Not only was there a substantial pay increase, but it also came with a rent-free luxury flat in Jessica's building and chauffeured luxury car at your disposal.

Since Jessica seemed to take care of herself, her assistant hardly did anything but run his or her own personal errands and answer a phone call every so often.

It was no wonder so many people applied. The applicants were pared down and only Peter and Monica were left standing. They'd acted out their own Spy vs. Spy series in the process.

Monica lobbed the first volley when she spiked Peter's tea with a few extra doses of Scotch before his presentation to the hiring committee. The gossip around the office was he'd been so sloshed, he forgotten how to speak English, although many at the presentation were impressed by his fluent German and Spanish.

Peter's response hadn't been as subtle. He emailed a few candid snapshots of Monica to the executive vice president of accounting, with a courtesy copy to the man's wife.

In other companies they would have been fired for their actions. Vixen's hiring committee actually recommended terminating them both, but Jessica vetoed the recommendation. She liked that her employees were fighting and going to the extremes to gain her approval. She told the committee to let Monica and Peter continue their shenanigans.

"To the victor belong the spoils," she'd remarked, and allowed the petty competition to continue.

Peter eventually emerged the victor, and Monica was left fuming at being passed over again. Though that hadn't stop her from proudly displayed her pearly whites every time Jessica was around.

"Monica," Jessica said. "Since you've been doing such a good job on these reports I would like you to sit in on the nine o'clock executive meeting. We're discussing potential marketing strategies and publicity options for Richmond's Sweets. I would like to hear some of your ideas."

"Yes, ma'am. Thank you, Ms. Paterson. I'll be more than happy to offer any assistance I can."

I sighed as I watched them stride down the corridor to the conference room—Jessica bulldozing her way and Monica sashaying behind her.

Once again, Monica had reaped the rewards for my work.

And once again, I was too much of a sad sap to stand up for myself. My office phone rang.

"Vixen Marketing, how can I direct your call," I answered, melancholy filling my thoughts.

I'm Karma Bailey, thirty-five and single. I'm not a high-powered CEO or wife to a handsome CFO. I have no children or any resemblance of the good life.

I am just a low-level, low-paid, bottom-feeder paper-pusher.

You know the saying about nice people finishing last?

Welcome to the real world, and in the real world, nice people don't even get picked for the team.

CHAPTER 2
IDIOT EXTRAORDINAIRE

I opened the door to the two-bedroom flat I shared with two flatmates. The place was located on the wrong side of the tracks and down the street from the liquor store that was conveniently located across the street from the neighborhood church.

To look at this place no one would ever believe that five years ago I was a senior-level financial research and analytics manager with one of the top firms in the country. Headhunted before leaving graduate school, my salary was slightly higher than the other senior-level managers. Honestly, I made more than my supervisor.

Of course that might explain why he had never liked me.

Despite my supervisor's antipathy toward me, the board of directors had seen me as a hard worker and placed me on the fast track to an executive-level position.

Achieving success in my chosen field hadn't been as easy as it sounded. Although I was smart with a near genius-level intelligence quotient, I'd been diagnosed with social anxiety disorder during a psychiatry session I had been forced to attend during my third year at university. The doctor prescribed medication that was supposed to help with my mood, but the side effects caused more ailments than the meds cured. I stopped taking the pills after a month and never attended another psychiatry session.

My job, however, required my attendance at various asinine social engagements and events. Because of my disorder, attending such events was extremely difficult. At one time I actually thought I had mastered the art of faking my emotions, like that television character Dexter.

It wasn't until after I vomited on my supervisor during the company's annual Christmas party I realized I hadn't quite mastered faking my emotions. My supervisor never forgot the incident and it only amplified his hatred toward me.

Notwithstanding the vomiting incident, my otherwise decent and high-paying career helped me afford the purchase of a beautiful, three-bedroom flat with a picturesque view of the city's skyline. Even with my large salary the place hadn't been cheap. I'd scraped and saved and paid off the mortgage in one year's time.

Now how does someone on the fast-track with a beautiful flat with a picturesque view of the city end up in a dump dodging drug addicts and pimps?

Suffice it to say that even with my near genius-level IQ and workaholic personality, I was still at times quite a daft cow. The head under my naturally jet-black hair held my intelligent brain and an over-abundance of book sense and Jeopardy-level knowledge.

But when common sense was dished out on creation day I must've been in the library with my nose stuck in a book. I'd also missed out on that injection of street smarts that would've warned me when people were only being my friend so they could take advantage of me.

Heck, even my own parents took advantage of my lack of common sense and my insatiable need to be liked. I hadn't realized it at the time though.

My parents were PhD professors who taught at universities all over the world. I developed my love of education, at the expense of any meaningful friendships, from the books they had bought me during their travels.

I'd spent hours in my room reading and doing homework for extra credit instead of socializing with other children. Since books didn't tease or bully me, I had found it safer to spend time with my imagination than with other people.

"Wonder where you'd be if they'd sent you a doll or a cheerleading outfit? Not living in some sorry ass flat with two slutty rejects from the Sex Parade."

My constant companion. How could I have forgotten about you?

You know that egotistical, insensible side of yourself that at times slipped out and said the most inappropriate rubbish at the most inappropriate time? I too had that side, and his name was Arrogance. He popped up whenever I was stressed, which was just about every minute of the day.

Arrogance was a very unsettling side effect of my social anxiety disorder, and he had been my constant companion since childhood.

Unlike normal people who were able to let that side of themselves out from time to time, I had never been able to let Arrogance take control, not even for a moment. No, Arrogance remained solely inside my head, where he happily dished out insults and ugliness every minute of the day.

Controlling Arrogance was a constant struggle. I admit there were times where I wished I could let him out in full force. But my unquenchable need to be liked and appreciated always won out. I supposed that's why Arrogance loved to torture me.

I hate Arrogance.

***

Back to how I ended up in the sewer pit of life. It happened one warm summer night about six-and-a-half years ago when Mum called. I should've known something was amiss because my parents never called when they were on their lecture tours — not even when I was a child.

Mum told me she and Dad were in Bruges. They'd been robbed and beaten while taking a romantic stroll around the city. They were in hospital and needed money to pay hospital bills and get a decent hotel until they recuperated. Could I send £5,000?

Arrogance screamed at me to tell her no. He told me to lie and tell her I don't have the money to send. Funny thing though, while Arrogance yelled in one ear, I could've sworn I heard another soft voice in my other ear that told me to hang up the phone right now.

I ignored both Arrogance and the other voice and sent the £5,000, with an extra £500 for a few clothes, food and other essentials.

Not a terrible story, right? A daughter helping her parents out of a jam, nothing wrong about that, right?

I didn't learn the truth until I came home two days later and found the cops ransacking my flat.

My parents were on an actual lecture circuit and were PhD professors who taught at universities. What I hadn't known was that their "lecture circuit" was actually a front for a drug smuggling ring. My parents for years had made their fortune as drug runners.

The cops, who weren't cops but government intelligence agents, explained Dad had been injured in Antwerp and taken to hospital, but it wasn't because my parents had been robbed.

Dad had crashed his car, but he'd done so trying to outrun the local police. The fact he was also a wee bit over the legal limit hadn't helped his cause much either.

That detail was just the tip of a Titanic-size iceberg!

When the police searched the vehicle, they found nearly sixty-five kilos of cocaine in various hideaways in the car. Apparently, Dad was supposed drive from Antwerp to Paris to meet up with his contact before he and mom boarded the Eurostar from Paris to London.

Dad, who always had a problem keeping his mouth shut when he was drunk, told the cops every detail. He even told the cops what color socks his contact wore.

The police rounded up all the low-level members of their drug ring over the next week. However, the top leaders had been tipped off and were long gone before the cops raided their hideouts.

The drug ring members, including my parents, were charged with everything the cops could fit onto the charge sheet. After a four-hour trial, my parents were convicted and sentence to twenty-five years in prison.

They never served a day.

While they waited for transport from the courthouse, a man wearing a black trench coat walked into the courthouse and started shooting everyone and everything in sight. The gunman was killed during the melee, and my parents had escaped during the chaos.

I remembered reading about the attack in the newspaper. Of course I, like most people, believed it to be a random 'lone wolf' attack. I learned from the government agents the attack wasn't random. My parents had used the £5,000 I sent them to pay some no-named wannabe gangster to shoot up the place.

The agents believed my parents were hiding out somewhere. Not only were they hiding from the law, but they were also hiding from the high-ranking drug kingpin they'd betrayed, and who now wanted my parents dead.

According to the agent assigned to my case, I had been kept under surveillance ever since my parents' arrest in the hope my parents would call or send me some sort of coded message.

So the faint voice I heard during the conversation with Mum was an agent trying to save me?

The agents continued their surveillance after I sent the money in the hope my parents would contact me again, giving the agents a chance to trace the call and pinpoint my parents' location.

Fat chance! My parents never called me or contacted me in any way since that night. Not even a "thank you, we got the money."

Of course the lack of contact hadn't stopped the agents from causing additional chaos in my life. When their surveillance hadn't brought the desired results, the agents questioned my co-workers, supervisor and my boss. They also put a freeze on my bank account.

The questioning and investigations led to me being sacked, though the official reason was because they were downsizing my entire department.

"What a load of bollocks," Arrogance had shrilled at the time.

If the loss of my job wasn't bad enough, I also lost my two friends whom I'd met in book club. Okay, so they weren't friends *per se*. We were more like nerds who got together and discussed romance and sci-fi novels. They both thought it was best to cut ties rather than endure continued harassment from government agents.

Books and work had been the only things that had helped keep my disorder manageable. Now both were gone.

The icing on the cake was the agents deciding to call off their surveillance of me a month after I'd been sacked. I thought that was a wee bit rude considering the fact that not only had their investigations led to me losing my job, but now some major drug kingpin might kill me as revenge for my parents' betrayal.

If I hadn't been depressed enough, one night about nine months after my parents' escape I received a call from a representative of Her Majesty's Revenue and Customs. The nice lady proceeded to tell me my parents had never paid taxes on the drug money.

"Are you freaking kidding me?" Arrogance was riled up and I struggled to control him. *"They really expect people to actually pay taxes on ill-gotten gains? Are they stupid?"*

"What does that have to do with me?" I asked the representative. My words escaped my mouth with a tad too much bluntness. The auditor picked up on that and took pleasure in informing me that my parents had used my information and identity to open multiple fraudulent credit accounts and establish dubious companies in my name to launder their ill-gotten gains.

"Guess you should've paid more attention to those free credit reports, huh?" Arrogance criticized.

Since the HMRC had no definitive proof I hadn't been involved in my parent's businesses, and since I hadn't alerted the credit card companies or banks about the fraudulent accounts, I was responsible for paying the debts accrued in my name.

I had no job, and the HMRC cleared out the money from all the accounts including my real checking account. They sold all my assets including my computers, laptops, furniture, appliances, video games systems, wardrobe and shoes.

They'd even auctioned my Beanie Babies collection.

"That one hurt," Arrogance cried at the time.

It was the seizure and auction of my condo that had hurt the most. The condo had been my fortress of solitude and last remaining asset. That loss sent me off the deep end of my depression. Sadness flowed through my veins and thoughts of suicide flooded my mind.

"I'm amazed you haven't slit your wrists or jumped off a building?" Arrogance said at the time.

Since I hadn't been able to afford the rent for a place of my own, I lived in Hannah's flat. Her twin sister, Alexis, lived here too and occupied the second bedroom. I slept on a sofa bed in their living room.

We'd attended the same secondary school. Hannah and Alexis were *those* girls. You know *those* girls — the beautiful, sexy and cool girls. They were the ones who'd always dressed in the latest slutty fashion, never paid attention in class, yet somehow managed to con teachers into giving them good marks. They were the girls who all the boys buzzed around every hour of the day. Hannah, Alexis and their clique had taken great pleasure in plucking those horny boys like guitar strings.

They'd also been part of the sorority who had bullied and torture nerdy girls like me.

They hadn't changed one bit over years. They still slept around, dressed liked slags and partied every night. And they still treated me like crap.

Hannah's flat reflected hers and Alexis's 'don't give a shite' attitude. The flat resided in a four-story building that housed five separate flats. Hannah's was the largest and occupied the entire top floor.

A top-floor flat in the city sounded amazing. That is until you saw the building. It was in shambles. Patches that did little more than keep the rain from drowning you in your sleep now held the once strong and steady roof together. It had been neglected for decades and was past its intended lifespan.

There was only one rickety staircase. The worn and beaten banister had broken years ago and was never fixed. The old lead paint that splattered the walls had chipped and peeled so much it resembled a dead body chalk outline; or was that a real chalk outline? In this neighborhood, no one could tell the difference. The truly sad part? No one cared.

Wild ivy contorted its way through a few broken windows. The other windows were boarded up, yet still had security bars. Outside lived drug addicts, pimps, wannabe gangsters and other ne'er-do-wells.

The building, notwithstanding its current ramshackle state, had been classified as a "listed building" some twenty years ago. It earned historic status because it had once been a beacon of hope and a leading stage for civil rights activities. It was also used as a safe haven for battered women and children a decade ago.

If the historical society saw the building now they'd drop dead from shock and dismay. Well that or dysentery from drinking the tap water.

There were five other people who lived in the building. Dave and Keith, a lovely couple in their mid-twenties, occupied one of the second-floor flats. Dave worked at the grocery store on the corner, and Keith was a dog walker. They'd always been polite to me, and I would exchange pleasantries, asking about their day whenever I saw them.

Janet and Nikki lived on the third floor. Janet was a flight attendant for one of those low-budget airlines, and Nikki worked at a local legal aid organization. Neither Janet nor Nikki got along with Hannah and Alexis. I heard Nikki once referred to them as *"STD-carrying lot lizards."* I never learned what that exactly meant, but I knew it wasn't an affectionate term.

On the first floor, in the flat marked 'Manager,' lived the building's horny toad — Mark. I couldn't stand the cheeky little bugger. Everyone in the building called him Professor Octopus.

The nickname wasn't because he'd been a marine biology professor during his younger days, but because he seemed to have tentacles everywhere. Whenever he got the chance he grabbed and squeezed women's butts as they passed. I apparently was an exception to his rule, because he'd never grabbed my bum.

I learned his little habit not only got him sacked from his last teaching job at a university up north, but it was also the reason for the large scar on the left side of his face. The story goes that Mark had groped a female student's arse and the girl's father, along a few of his friends, had beaten Mark to a bloody pulp. Mark checked himself out of hospital later that day and hightailed it out of town. He didn't even go back to his place to pack a bag or feed his fish.

Except for the occasional gossip here and there everyone tended to mind his or her own business. Since I wasn't a sociable person that had suited me just fine.

Yet I would always wonder what they said about me behind my back.

I walked into the kitchen and put my groceries away, then I sat down on the living room sofa, which doubled as my bed.

I had been force to sell most of my belongings to pay off the debts, so didn't have a need for a full bedroom. Hannah and Alexis were quite happy to remind me of that fact every day.

I was about to call it a day and watch the rest of *Bridget Jones' Diary* when the front door swung open and hit the wall with a loud bang.

Hannah stumbled in drunk, stinking of cigarettes and cheap cologne. Some bloke followed her in. His hands groped and squeezed her butt as he slobbered all over her neck. I watched them grope each other on their way to Hannah's bedroom. Their loud sucking sounds, and Hannah's fake *"yeah daddy, right there,"* made me want to puke. When they came up for air the guy noticed me watching them from the couch.

"Hey, thought you said you had the place to yourself," the chap said.

"I do," Hannah replied. She twisted around so fast she almost fell on her rear. The guy caught her and held her up.

"Oh, her?" Hannah said, pointing at me. "Oh, don't mind her, she's nobody. C'mon lover boy, my room is over there."

She grabbed the guy's arm, pulled him into her room and slammed the door. I could hear them going at it. Hannah's fake *"oh yeah, oh yeah, that's it, right there,"* was awful. It was so obvious she was faking it.

"Jealous much, are we?" Arrogance asked.

I sighed and pushed *play* on the remote.

This is my life. One big cosmic joke.

Will tomorrow be any different?

Will I suddenly get everything in life I ever wanted?

Only in my dreams.

CHAPTER 3
A REAL SHOCK

My alarm's kitty-cat buzzer shrieked at exactly 6:30 in the morning.

"Oh, Jiminy Cricket," I yelp and jumped out of bed. I needed to be at work by eight, and it took an hour by subway to get to the office. A taxi would've been much quicker, but the £60 fare would put my monthly budget over the max. No, a cab was out of the question.

I rushed to get ready and headed to the bathroom. It was locked, so I knocked on the door.

"What," Hannah yelled.

"Will you be long?" I asked. "I'm going to be late for work."

Hannah opened the door. She had on my bathrobe. I said nothing.

"How's that my fucking problem? Besides doesn't your office have a gym? Take a shower there," Hannah said.

"Hey babe you gonna join me or what?" Hannah's date from last night asked. Hannah pushed me away from the door.

"Get lost, spaz. Can't you see I'm busy?" She slammed the door in my face.

I headed back to my room. Suddenly the bathroom door opened and Hannah stuck her head out.

"Since you're in such a rush, here take these!" She threw a package of body wipes at me. The package hit me in the forehead.

Hannah laughed and slammed the door shut.

I picked up the wipes and crushed them in anger but I held my tongue. Why can't I just tell her off? Heck why can't I tell everybody off?

"Because you're a sap, duh."

I ignored Arrogance and glanced at my watch. Oh crud! It was 6:45 a.m. I rushed back into my bedroom and dressed in the plain-looking black pants suit I found at the charity shop around the corner.

My monthly budget — stretched as far as I could stretch it — would never allowed for shopping sprees at high-end boutiques or even the moderate department stores. I shopped wherever my meager funds allowed and that usually meant the local charity shops.

Hannah had loaned me a privacy screen. I thought she was being nice. She said she only gave me the darn thing so none of her boy-toys would vomit at the sight of me. I finished dressing and had just enough time to pack my lunch and get to the subway.

I'd just stuffed a tuna sandwich into brown paper bag, along with a fruit punch-flavored juice box and an apple, when the door to Alexis' bedroom opened. Alexis stepped out, yawned and stretched.

"Good morning, Alexis," I said. "Hey, the electric bill needs to be paid, and I won't have time to pay it. Can you take care if of it this month? Oh and I have the receipt here for the dry cleaning you asked me to pick up the other day. If you could repay me for that it would really hel—"

"Yea, yea, yea," Alexis cut me off. Suddenly, a handsome stud grabbed Alexis by the waist. She let out a small yelp and chuckled.

"Where's my sexy nurse going, hmm?" the stud asked. "Your patient needs another rubdown."

"Another rubdown? I think someone's due for a sponge bath," Alexis replied. She stroked the stud's groin and he moan. "Who's that," the stud moaned.

"Her?" Alexis responded. "Oh, don't mind her, she's nobody." Alexis gently pushed the stud back into her room and slammed the door.

I stood in the kitchen and stared at the closed door.

"You know she's not going to repay you, right?" Arrogance admonished. *"Karma, sometimes you're such a sorry piece of —"*

"Hey, thought you were in a hurry to get to work," Hannah interrupted Arrogance's insult. She had just come out the loo and headed toward her bedroom. Her date followed her like a sad lap dog.

I checked the clock. It was 7:15. Oh fudge! I was going to be really late. I checked my wallet for my Oyster card and found £60 missing from my purse.

Funny, I knew I had it yesterday. Maybe Alexis or Hannah borrowed it and forgotten to tell me.

I stuffed my laptop into my bag, grabbed my lunch and my coat and rushed out of the flat. I glanced at my watch when I got outside. It was 7:45. I would have to take a cab if I stood any chance of getting to work on time. I held up my hand and yelled for a taxi. The cab pulled to a stop. I'd opened the door and was about to get in when I remembered the missing £60.

Bollocks! I had no cash to pay for the cab. I would have to take the tube. I apologized to the cab driver. He cursed and called me a bitch as he drove off. Guess I wasn't the only one who woke up on the wrong side of the bed this morning.

I broke the heel on one of my shoes running to the station. I thought luck was on my side since I had barely caught the express train and arrived at work at two minutes passed eight. I collapsed in my desk chair and hoped no one noticed my slight tardiness.

That bubble burst the moment I heard the stomps of a 300-pound hippo, the flapping of a thrift store muumuu and the smacking of fruity gum, for that meant my supervisor was on her way toward my desk to chastise me.

"About time you got here," Mary said.

Mary St. Charles.

Mary was my obese, ugly wig-wearing, bad-breath-having supervisor. Seriously she was fatter than Santa Claus and less jolly, except when she and her posse tormented me. She stood next to my desk and tapped her watch.

"You're late," she reprimanded. "I'm docking your pay."

"You're docking me fifteen percent for two minutes," I cried. "Please I can't afford to have less pay this month."

"Should've thought about that before you showed up late."

"Can't I make it up? Stay a little past my normal time?"

"Work begins at eight and ends at five. No excuses. You're not at your desk at eight sharp, you get docked fifteen percent."

I watched Mary waddled back to her desk. Although she weighed about 300 pounds, most of it was in her butt. She was a bitter, cynical and very irritating she-devil — at least toward me anyway.

I watched as she stopped by the supply cabinet on her way to her desk and grabbed a few boxes of pens and sticky notes.

I sighed and pulled out my ruler. I straighten my penholder and then measured it to ensure it was exactly six inches from my laptop and exactly six inches from the edge. I then booted up my laptop. The startup sing-sing tune had just sounded when Karen, another secretary, walked in.

I glanced at the clock and so did Mary. It was 8:45.

"You're late, Karen," Mary called out.

"Sorry, Mary — hot date last night," Karen replied.

"Really? Well, I'll let it slide" Mary said, "as long as I get to hear the juicy details at lunch."

"What the fudge," Arrogance barked. *"You were two minutes late and got fifteen percent of your pay docked. Yet Miss Sexually-Transmitted Disease walks in forty-five late and Mary lets it slide? Karma when are you gonna grow a pair and —"*

I muted Arrogance and just glared at Karen and Mary while they talked about Karen's latest adventure. When Karen turned and headed back to her desk, I saw Mary put the boxes of pens and sticky notes into her purse.

What a worthless kleptomaniac. Mary stole some sort of office supply every day. Today it was pens and sticky pads. Yesterday it was staples. No, not the stapler and staples, just the staples.

"What a tosser," Arrogance mocked. *"If you're gonna risk getting sacked for theft, at least steal something worth it — like the petty cash box or a laptop. Am I right? I'm right, huh?"*

I shook my head and went back to my daily routine.

"You need to go on a coffee run," Mary said.

I hadn't noticed when she approached my desk, but her foul

breath nearly knocked me out of my seat the second her mouth opened.

"Geez, what did she have to drink this morning? A Grande-size up of piss?" Arrogance gagged.

Mary handed me a list of coffee orders. I logged off my laptop and grabbed my purse.

"Before you head out, you might want to make use of these," she said and tossed me the package of baby wipes. The package must have dropped from my bag when I pulled the laptop out.

Then — in a loud voice so everyone in the office heard — Mary shouted "my god! You smell like dog shit."

Everyone laughed. A few people fanned the air in front them, waving away the non-existed odor, as Mary added, "you smell worse than a three-day old dirty nappy."

Mary laughed and headed back to her desk. I noticed that Karen, along with everyone else in our section, laughed right along with Mary. I stuffed the baby wipes into my bag. I felt the heat rising in my cheeks and prayed no one noticed.

I coughed and tried to stop my tears from falling down my face. Having ten of your co-workers, and one or two mid-level managers, laughing and pointing fingers at you because your supervisor just lied about you having a hygiene problem was beyond humiliating. It was mortifying and distressing. I hurried to the lifts, rushing passed Karen as I went.

"There she goes," Karen sang. "Make way for Ms. *Stank-Kay.*"

Everyone laughed. I lowered my head to my chest and continued to the lifts. I went to the second-level, where the gym was located, and into the toilet, and straight to the third stall. I always went to the third stall in a public toilet. I know, statistically, the toilet closest to the entrance was usually cleaner, but I always went to the third stall. I angrily slammed my hands against the stall door three or four times before I placed a paper cover sheet on the toilet and crumpled onto the toilet.

There I sat — on a smelly toilet someone forgot to flush — and cried. Since the day I started work here — I'd experienced a seemingly never-ending course of bullying, teasing, humiliation and verbal torture. Every single day!

"Why is this always a surprise to you?" Arrogance began. *"It has happened every day of your life — every day since primary school. You always asked 'why me?' That's easy! You're afraid of your own shadow. People like Mary are like dogs. They can smell fear. You simply become a target for them to vent their frustrations on and feel superior. They know you won't do anything to stop them. No — you'll just sit on some smelly toilet and take it."*

Arrogance, in his own mean and spiteful way, was right. People like Mary were quick to pick up on my fears, my shyness and my social awkwardness. He was also right that I would do nothing to stop them.

I had tried once, about a year or two ago. I filed a complaint with Employee Relations about Mary's treatment of me. Unfortunately for me, Mary got wind of the complaint from Lily.

Lily was the division manager for department's employee grievances section. She was also Mary's BFF. Two days after I filed my complaint, I was told there was evidence that my complaint was fraudulent, and nothing more than retaliation after receiving an unfavorable work evaluation from Mary.

As part of my reprimand I received no annual bonus that year and lost two weeks of vacation time. The company also cut my salary five percent and warned that if another complaint was received about me, or if I file another complaint that was determined to be fraudulent, my employment would be terminated.

So here I sat, on a stinky toilet, unable to do anything but cry.

***

It had been a week since the baby wipe incident. Things continued as normal, and I continued to be bullied both at home and work.

It was Friday. I hated Fridays.

But today wasn't just any Friday, either. Oh no! Today was a payday Friday.

This morning began as others always did — another clutter of chaos. First, my alarm hadn't sounded, which was weird because I know I set it before I went to sleep last night. When I checked it, I found it unplugged.

I had to take a cold shower since there was no hot water.

Then I discovered my stockings had a run in them and I didn't have another pair. I had to buy another pair at the little stand next to the tube station, which meant I paid triple what I would've paid at a department store.

I'd missed the express train and had to take the regional. The only good thing to happen this morning was I had remembered to grab my lunch, a tuna fish sandwich and celery sticks, before I dashed out the flat.

I sat on the train and glanced at people going about their business. Everyone seemed more or less happy. They looked forward to the weekend and their fun. Two women talked about how they were gonna spend their weekly paycheck getting "rejuvenated" at some new wellness spa. Three guys standing near the door chatted about the upcoming football matches they plan were planning to attend. A group of teenage girls flipped through a tween magazine and gabbed on about the members of some new boy band. Everyone had such glee and joy in their voices that I almost felt happy for them, and I almost smiled.

Then someone spilt their nasty white mocha Frappuccino on me. Reality has a funny sense of timing, doesn't it? I heard Arrogance's laughter as I wiped the sticky mess off my blouse.

I arrived at work one minute late. Of course Mary quite happily docked my pay.

Later that morning while I sat at my desk, my thoughts drifted again. I sat there and tried to understand the happiness effect that came with payday Fridays.

Most people look forward to paydays and Fridays. On principle I understood the feeling. For ordinary blokes, Friday meant freedom. The weekend was only a few hours away, and then two days of bliss before the dread and gloom of Monday morning reared its head again.

For me, Friday meant two days away from work, which was the only thing besides books that brought me any comfort. For me, Fridays blows. They always had and they always would.

Plus, ever since my parents' debauchery, I especially hated payday Fridays. The amount of my paycheck — what was left of it after the HMRC, the credit card companies and the banks had taken their cut — left me barely enough to pay my share of the rent and buy food.

There was one thing I hated more than payday Friday and that was lunchtime on a payday Friday!

While everyone talked about their weekend plans, I'd sit at my normal table in the lunchroom, the one in the corner away from the laughing eyes of my coworkers, and silently eat my lunch.

Today, there were two other people in the lunchroom when I entered, Gail and Tom. Gail worked in accounting, Tom in legal. They sat at their normal table in the center of the room. As usual they were engaged in a deep debate about some new tax law. They were among the very few people in the company who actually said hello to me when they saw me.

Most people never realized how much a simple "hello" could brighten the darkest day in a person's life.

I returned the greeting, then grabbed my lunch from the fridge. I sat at my normal table and went through my lunchtime preparation routine.

First, I'd wiped down the table with one of my four moist towelettes. Then I carefully unfolded my paper napkin and placed it on my lap. On the table, I placed my plastic fork on the left; my knife and spoon on the right. I opened my bottled water and took a quick sip to cleanse my palette, then placed the bottle to my right and six inches away from the edge of the table.

I punched the straw through the juice box's tiny tinfoil-covered hole and sat the box to my left. I used my plastic knife to cut my sandwich in half, diagonally. Then, using another napkin, I wiped the knife clean before I returned it to its spot next to the spoon.

No, I do not have Obsessive-Compulsive Disorder. I simply tried to maintain a standard daily routine because, well because things just had to be done in a certain way in order for me to function.

"Yeah, you don't have OCD," Arrogance mocked. *"Yeah, and Elvis is still alive and living in a commune in Peru."*

I muted Arrogance for the moment and concentrated on my peanut butter sandwich. The preparation routine always ended with my saying grace. After all that had happened to me over the past five years, I had no qualms in saying my faith in God was practically eradicated. However, habit obligated me to say grace before taking a bite of my food.

I was mid-chew when Mary, Karen and Tasha entered the lunchroom. Tasha was Monica's BFF and the administrative assistant for the head of the graphics department.

Tasha and Monica normally ate lunch together. The fact she was with Mary and Karen only meant one thing — Monica was out *"servicing"* a client.

Wait, today was Friday. Monica usually reserved Fridays for Vixen's executives and senior managers. She was probably in some janitor's closet with her skirt hiked up around her waist, and straddling some balding, and married, executive.

"OMG! Ladies, what's that smell?" Karen mocked when she saw me. She fanned the air in front of her. "Oh it's Ms. *Stank-Kay.*"

Gail and Tom momentarily stopped their conversation, and Gail gave Karen a look of disgust. Other than that, Gail and Tom ignored the posse and resumed their conversation a few seconds later.

"My god," Mary chimed in. "Have some common decency, *Stank-Kay*. People eat in here." Karen snatched up one of my moist towelettes and wiped her hands with it. She balled the tiny cloth up and feigned like she was going to throw it into the trash. Instead, she threw the dirty cloth in my face, then took the other half of my sandwich and gobbled it down.

Karen, Tasha and Mary laughed. They grabbed their lunches from the fridge and sat down at their normal table by the window. They always sat there so they could look out and judge the men who walked past.

They gave the men grades ranging from *"mama should've left him on someone's doorstep,"* to *"I'd do him,"* to the oh-so-clever *"he's so ugly the only girl he'd get is Karma."*

They laughed, ate and gossiped on about inner-office relationships.

"Did you hear about Maggie from media and Jack from IT?" Karen asked.

"No," Mary and Tasha said together.

"Well, I heard they were getting it on in the third-floor supply closet. In fact, everyone on the third floor heard them getting it on," Karen laughed. Tasha joined in.

I gathered the remains of my lunch and swept the crumbs into a napkin and walked over to the trash. As I tossed the trash into the bin, it was only then that I remembered I hadn't packed a peanut butter sandwich for lunch. I had packed tuna.

I was so deep in thought about payday Fridays I'd mistakenly grabbed someone else's lunch by mistake. I checked the wadded up brown lunch bag to see if it had a name on it. I only hoped the person would accept my apology and my offer to reimburse them. I also hoped that person wouldn't report me to Employee Relations for theft. That would certainly ensure my employment termination. I checked the bag. There was no name on it.

"Girl that's old news," Mary said. Her loud mouth interrupted my thoughts.

"Now, I heard that a secretary in legal got down and dirty with a senior-level executive from Weist Financial," Mary continued. "And when I say down, I mean *way down*."

"Who?" Tasha asked. She sat with her mouth gaped like some school slut who couldn't wait to hear about the football star and the science teacher.

Sadly, I felt the same way. I stood by the trashcan and waited for Mary to identify the executive. As she leaned in to tell the others, I unconsciously leaned in as well.

"Well, my sources told me —"

"What the hell are you doing *Stank-Kay*," Karen shouted. She caught me listening and was now about to unleash the full force of her nastiness on me. "You little turd-wipe. Always in other's people's business aren't you?"

As she yelled at me, I noticed she scratched at her arm and tears formed in her eyes. She wiped her eyes but kept scratching her arm.

"Yeah, you should get your sorry arse back to work before I dock you for being late from lunch," Mary chimed in.

"Better yet she needs to take her *Stank-Kay* arse to the nearest shower and wash that funk off," Tasha jumped in and fanned the air with her hand. "Crikey, you smell worse than fresh dog shit."

The three women laughed. I turned away and rushed toward

the exit so they wouldn't see the tears that began to fall from my eyes. I had just reached the door when I heard Karen begin to cough.

"Damn, girl, the joke wasn't that funny," Tasha said.

Karen tried to say something but her breath caught in her throat. It took a few seconds before anyone realized she was choking. She doubled over and gasped for air.

"What's wrong with you, girl?" Mary asked.

"Oh, god, she's choking," Tasha said in a panic. "Somebody help her!"

Neither I, Tom or Gail moved. I wouldn't say our unwillingness to move was due to some thoughts of minding our own business. I know I didn't move because shock momentarily controlled my body and prevented me from doing anything but stare — like people do when passing an auto accident on the motorway.

Karen jerked upright for a second. She grabbed her throat and fell— face-first and hard — onto the floor. Mary and Tasha screamed, and that finally broke the shroud that held my other co-workers. Tom rushed over to help. Gail dialed 999.

"She must be having an allergic reaction," Tom screamed. He turned Karen over onto her back and checked her pulse. When I saw her face, I nearly lost my lunch.

Her face was a tinged blue and her eyes looked as if they were ready to burst out of her skull. Tom opened her mouth to give her CPR, but Karen's tongue was so swollen I doubted he would have much success giving her mouth-to-mouth.

Our screams and noise attracted more people to the lunchroom. Someone brought a Ready Rescue Response kit and helped Tom perform CPR. Other people just stood and watched. Only a minute had passed and Karen still didn't show signs that the CPR was working.

"Paramedics are on the way," Gail yelled. "They said to keep doing CPR. They want to know if there's an EpiPen in her purse. Does she have an EpiPen?"

Mary and Tasha stood holding each other.

"Do you know if she has her EpiPen?" Gail yelled at them.

"No, I ... I" Mary stammered. "I don't know."

Gail turned to me. I shrugged and shook my head.

"Where's her purse?" Gail questioned Tasha. Tasha gazed at Gail but didn't respond.

"She locked it in her desk. She didn't think she would need it since we weren't leaving the building," Mary replied.

"I'm still not getting a pulse and she is not breathing," Tom yelled. He continued CPR.

Five minutes had passed by the time the medics arrived. They checked Karen's pulse and her pupils. They worked fast, got her onto the stretcher and rolled her out. Tasha and Mary followed the medics, holding each other as they rushed out.

Although they performed all their steps and protocol, and had not said a word to anyone as they rolled Karen out the door, I saw the look in one of the medics' eyes confirming what I thought.

Karen was dead.

***

Frank Willis, Vixen's executive vice-president of employee relations, broke the news to everyone two hours later. After a quick speech about how Karen was a valuable member of the team and will be sorely missed, he announced that grief counselors would be available to anyone who needed to talk.

Willis added the company would allow individuals attending Karen's funeral to take three hours off work, with pay, to attend the service.

Of course, individuals had to clear it with their supervisors first. Guess I won't be attending the service. There's no way Mary would approve my request.

I sat at my desk and continued my work. I watched as Willis bee-lined toward Mary and Tasha when they returned to the office. He gave the same speech he just gave to the rest of us. The tears fell from Mary's and Tasha's eyes. Willis hugged them both.

He whispered something to them. They whispered their answer then nodded towards me. Willis nodded and said something. Then he hugged them both again and walked to the lifts. As he past me his eyes shot daggers at me.

Why had he looked at me like that?

"Are you sure you graduated from Oxford?" Arrogance smirked. *"I*

think it's time to get that CV up-to-date. Better yet, you might want to find a cheap solicitor."

***

Everyone knew it was an allergic reaction that killed Karen. Nevertheless, the police wanted to question me, Tom, Gail, Mary and Tasha since we had been in the lunchroom when Karen had collapsed.

Standard police procedure, from what I was told, even when the police thought the incident was simply an accident. I felt it was more of the company's way of protecting itself from a lawsuit. Thirty minutes after the workday ended, I was summoned to the fifth floor conference room.

Detective Inspector Damian Harris introduced himself and his partner, Detective Constable Alastair Eason. I was troubled by the fact they'd waited until the end of the day to interview me. The others had been interviewed and had gone home already.

So why am I still here? And why had they interviewed the others before me? I wondered if Willis had given them the impression I was totally responsible for what happened to Karen.

"So, Miss...?" DI Harris inquired.

"Bailey," I replied. "Karma Bailey."

"Ms. Bailey, this is an informal interview, but I am required to inform you that you have the right, if you so choose, to have a solicitor present during the interview. If so, we can postpone this interview and conduct it later at the station."

"I understand, and I don't think I need legal representation," I replied.

"Okay. Remember, you can request a lawyer at any time," DC Eason reminded me. I smiled.

I could tell DI Harris didn't approved of Eason telling me that by the way he sucked loudly on that darn lollipop.

"Right. Now that we're done with the formalities, tell us what happened in the lunchroom today?" he barked.

He sat on the edge of the conference room table and continued to suck loudly on a lollipop.

"Does he really think he's Kojak?" Arrogance angrily questioned. *"Or is he trying to draw attention to his lips? He shouldn't bring any*

attention to those dry and crusty things. Ever heard of ChapStick genius?"

I glanced at DC Eason. He stood behind his partner, notepad and pen in hand ready to jot down my statement. He smiled just enough to show a gleam of brilliant white and perfectly aligned teeth. My heart skipped a beat. His smile put me at ease and helped me relax. I felt safe.

Then I looked back at Harris and those crusty lips and cringed. I lowered my head slightly so I wouldn't have to look at those lips and recounted what happened in the lunchroom.

"So, if I understand correctly, you offered Ms. Greene a bite of your sandwich? Did you know of Ms. Greene's allergies?"

"I didn't know her that well. We weren't exactly friends," I replied. He and Eason glanced at each other. They both looked puzzled. I guessed Mary and Tasha had convinced them that we had all been friends some time ago, before I turned into the office antichrist. Since we'd been friends I would've known about Karen's allergy when I offered her a bite of my sandwich, though I never offered her anything.

"So you had no prior knowledge of Ms. Greene's allergies?"

"No."

"If you two weren't exactly friends why did you offer her a bite of your sandwich?"

I had opened my mouth to address his claim when the door opened. Vince, one of the company's IT specialist, backed in. He was pulling a computer cart loaded with equipment, cables and various tools. He jumped when he saw us. DC Eason calmly walked over and prevented Vince from coming any farther into the room.

"Oh, I'm sorry," Vince said. "I didn't know anyone was in here. I was just about to setup for tomorrow's meeting."

"Find another room! I'm conducting an interview here," Harris said and flashed his badge. Vince backed out and DI Harris returned his attention to my interrogation. Eason shut the door.

"Now, when you first noticed Ms. Greene was having difficulties, I understand you made no attempt to offer any aid at all to help her. Is that correct?" Harris continued the questioning.

"Yes. I made no attempt to offer any assistance."

"Is there a reason why?"

At that very moment Arrogance rose up and made a very serious attempt to knockout my rational side.

"Listen you self-righteous, pompous, cheap-cologne-wearing vagabond," Arrogance shouted. *"No I didn't help her. I stood where I was and tried not to bust a gut as I laughed and said 'that's what you get, you trollop!'"*

Terrified of what would have happened if I let Arrogance take over, even for a minute, I went with the classic, and safer, response.

"I don't know. I ... I was too scared to move sir," I stammered. "I guess I was in shock or something."

"Hmm, I can understand that," Eason interjected. "It was a very frightening scene. Was that the only reason? It wasn't because you two weren't the best of friends."

I shook my head. He stared at me and waited for me to say more. His beautiful blue eyes displayed a softness and caring sweetness, with a touch of shyness that sent unexpected warmth through me. I shook that thought from my brain and answered the question.

"We weren't friends but we were professional to each other at work," I lied. "I'm sorry she died and even more sorry I didn't do more to help her." I hoped this would end any further interrogation. "Is there anything else, sir? I really need to get home."

"No. No. Nothing, you can go. I may have questions later, though, so don't leave town anytime soon, all right?" Harris said. He licked his lips at me. He thought it was very sexy and seductive. It wasn't sexy or seductive — it was sickening.

I took two deep breaths to compose myself, then nodded and left the room. I walked back to my desk and grabbed my bag, laptop and coffee mug and walked to the lifts. As I passed Karen's desk, I glanced at the mass of cards and flowers that had suddenly covered it.

"You were such a lovely person and you will be missed," read one card.

"Can't believe you're gone. This place won't be the same without you," read one next to a bouquet of white lilies.

"You were so beautiful, caring and thoughtful. Always there to lend a helping hand," read another.

I scoffed and continued on my way.

"You should've taken a big dump all over her desk," Arrogance reprimanded.

CHAPTER 4
ONE EPIC PLUNGE

I missed my regular train and got home around eight. Winter had come early and the weather report predicted a snowstorm would hit later tonight.

The whole way home I couldn't control my thoughts about Karen and about how I had grabbed the wrong lunch. I closed my eyes and leaned my head back against the seat. I tried to settle my thoughts a little. But I couldn't help but remember how I just stood there and watched as Karen struggled for breath.

Why hadn't I helped? Why had I just stood there? Had I wanted this to happen? Was that the reason I'd grabbed the wrong lunch bag? On some subconscious level, had I really wanted to hurt Karen?

"Of course you wanted to hurt her, duh." Arrogance tormented me all the way home and didn't let up as I walked up the stairs to the flat. I shook my head in a misguided attempt to oust his hateful thoughts from my mind. I opened the door, walked in and proceeded to trip over the welcome mat.

"Darn it, Alexis," I said and set my laptop bag to the floor next to the sofa.

Alexis had bought the stupid mat because she fancied herself as an interior decorator. It was an ugly shag carpet thing straight from the 1950s. Every day at least one of us tripped on the loose threading.

"Alexis, that damn mat is going to kill someone one of these days," Hannah once yelled at Alexis. Hannah had tripped over the mat and spilt her precious $7 Cafe Misto with Soy, which in Hannah's world was worse than high treason.

I flicked the light switch next to the door. Nothing happened. I flicked the switch off, then on. Again nothing.

Oh, fudge! Alexis hadn't paid the bill and now we had no electricity. After the events of today, and with a snowstorm on its way, no electricity or heat meant this would be a long weekend. In the darkness, I stumbled my way to Alexis's room.

"Alexis," I yelled as I threw open the door. I immediately wished I hadn't done so.

The stench of semen, love juice and days-old Chinese food hit my nose and made my eyes water. The strawberry-scented candle hadn't done anything to mask the odor. The bed was unmade and covered with mini-skirts and pantyhose. A half-eaten baloney and cheese sandwich laid on top of a chipped purple plate, which was now stuck to the nightstand. Next to the plate laid two empty bottles of cheap wine.

The small metal wastebasket was filled with empty condom wrappers, Chinese food cartons, and pizza boxes. It pleaded for a fresh trash liner. The closet door was open, and I saw a mountain of mini-skirts, designer dresses and short-shorts under a pile of stilettos of various heights.

"Good gracious me," I blurted.

"See, I told you! I told you! I told you she has been stealing from me. What the hell are you doing in my room?" Alexis shouted from behind me.

In a state of pure bewilderment and horror at the state of her room, I hadn't realized she or Hannah were home. Hannah stood next to her and shined a flashlight in my face.

"Sorry, Alexis. I was coming to ask you —" I began.

"Save the drama," she shouted. "I told you Hannah. She stole my money, that's why I didn't pay the electric bill."

I stood there baffled. Alexis just accused me of stealing her money? She'd been stealing my money, not vice versa.

"Karma, Alexis said you've been stealing from her for a couple of months now," Hannah accused. "Now she's missing

£200. She said it was in her purse. When she checked this morning after you left for work the money was gone."

"I didn't take her money," I cried.

"You thieving bitch," Alexis screamed. "You stole that money out of my purse! That's why you were in my room ain't it! You were looking for more and didn't think we'd be home now!"

"I didn't take your money."

"C'mon Karma just admit it! You stole the money," Hannah yelled. "We caught you red-handed!"

Alexis shoved me hard against the living room wall. "Bitch give me back my damn money now! I know you got it." She grabbed my laptop bag, turned it upside down and shook everything out onto the floor, including the company's laptop.

"Where's my money?"

"I haven't stolen a thing from you," I countered. "I only went into your room because I thought you were in here and I wanted to ask why you hadn't paid the electric bill."

"That's shite," Hannah refuted.

"It's the truth. I asked Alexis last week to pay the bill."

"You fuckin' liar. You never asked me a damn thing and you know it," Alexis replied.

"Look Karma —" Hannah began. She took a deep breath before she continued. "We tried to be nice and all, especially after all you've been through, but this is the last straw. I don't want to involve the police —"

"Call the cops Hannah. Just call them. She's nothing but a thief just like her parents. At least her parents were good at it."

The mention of my parents being good thieves sparked fury I hadn't known I possessed.

Smack!

I slapped the taste out of Alexis' mouth. Alexis reeled back and held her cheek in her hand. Hannah just stood there. She was as shocked by my outburst as I was.

Alexis wasn't shocked, however. She was furious. She screeched and then jumped at me. She grabbed me by the hair and slammed me against the wall again. She punched me twice in the gut. Pain jolted throughout my body. My stomach ached, I lost feeling in my arms and my legs began to weaken. I gasped and grabbed my stomach as I sunk to the floor.

It was weird, but as I lay on the floor I actually saw that little spark of mine slowly fade. As it flamed out, so too did my willingness to fight back.

Alexis stood over me. She kicked me once more, then screeched, "You lying bitch. I always pay my share. You're nothing but a lying slag and a thief. Hannah I told ya. You shouldn't have let this bitch move in. She's nothing but a bloody thief and a lying sack of shite." Hannah finally stepped in and stopped Alexis from kicking me again.

"Alexis, that's enough," Hannah shouted. "That's enough." She turned to me. "Karma we know you stole the money. You gotta go."

"No don't do this," I blubbered. "I haven't stolen any money. Believe me, it's the truth."

"Look, it's not just the money. Other things, small things, have also come up missing," Hannah continued. "Alexis was right. I shouldn't have let you move in here, especially not after learning about your parents, that government crap and everything. We tried being nice and all, but now you've blown it. We don't trust you anymore. Since we don't trust you, you can't live here anymore."

"Please," I begged.

"You've got five minutes. Get your stuff and leave or I'll call the police."

I struggled to get to my feet. Darn, my stomach hurt. The tears spilled down my face. "But I have nowhere to go."

"That's not our bloody problem, bitch," Alexis shouted. "You got four minutes. Hurry the fuck up!"

Slowly, I stuffed my clothes into my suitcase as I gingerly held my stomach. I picked up my laptop bag and stuffed it inside, noticing a small crack on the computer case as I did. Since it was a company laptop and signed out to me, I would be responsible for paying to have it repaired.

I pleaded one more time for Hannah to reconsider. Her face told me to get out now. Tears fell from my eyes as I walked to the door. Alexis followed me step-for-step. I wondered if she would literally kick me out.

My hands and arms were full so I set the laptop bag on the floor next to the door before I opened it. I carried my suitcase down the stairs first and set that by the entrance. When I turned to head back up the stairs to grab my box of toiletries and the laptop bag, Alexis was blocking the flat's doorway. She held the computer bag in her hand.

"Hey bitch, don't forget this," she shouted. She swung the bag back and forth. I freaked, quickly realizing what Alexis planned to do.

"Alexis, please don't," I cried. She laughed and swung her arm back, ready to toss my bag.

What happened next would remain etched into my memory for my lifetime.

As Alexis's arm swung forward, her big toe caught one of the loose threads in the welcome mat. She stumbled and dropped the laptop bag. She tried to catch herself and keep from falling, but she failed. Her stocking feet didn't helped her cause either.

She fell forward. Time stopped as she flew through the air, flapping her arms like they were wings.

Gravity was quick to remind her she was no bird.

Had the stairs been carpeted like the ones in my old flat her plummet might not have been so bad. But this was a historic building. The stairs were concrete and unforgiving.

Alexis' arms and hands flailed in search something, or someone to grab onto. Her plunge toward the bottom ended with a sickening crack as her head bounced of the concrete at the foot of the steps.

Landing face-up, her right leg twisted unnaturally under her body. Her left hand was broken in numerous places. Her eyes were wide opened and lifeless. Blood poured from every orifice and pooled on the floor around her.

The incident had lasted no more than ten seconds, but it had felt like forever. And like earlier today with Karen, I stood frozen, unable to do anything but watch.

Hannah appeared in the doorway. "What the hell is going?" she shouted. "Karma, why the fuck are you still here?"

I didn't respond.

"Karma, answer me. Why are you still—?" Her words caught

in her throat when she noticed Alexis now lay in a broken heap at the bottom of the stairs.

"Oh, my god. Alexis!" She rushed down the steps. She pushed me out of her way and dropped to her knees. She screamed and cradled Alexis's head in her arms.

"Alexis," she shouted. "For god's sake, someone help! Help! Someone help! Karma what the fuck did you do?"

"What the hell is going on out here," Mark yelled and stepped out from his flat. "You slags need to shut the hell—!"

His eyes nearly bulged out of his head. "Holy fucking Jesus! What the hell happened?" He pulled his mobile from his pocket and dialed 999. He had to yell into the phone in order for the operator to hear him over Hannah's screams.

The commotion and screams brought Keith and Dave out from their flat. After a quick survey of the scene, they rushed over to Hannah and Alexis. Dave tried to pull Hannah off Alexis so that Keith could provide some basic medical aid. I slowly moved up to the middle of the stairway and stood and watched.

I didn't make any attempt to help. I just stared at Alexis. A strangeness like never before took over my body. I felt no breeze. I heard not one sound, neither close nor far. My breath trapped inside my body and my arms were glued to my sides.

What was really weird though? I wasn't traumatized or had any feeling of sorrow. In fact, I felt an eerie sense of serenity. It was a sort awe-inspiring easiness with the loneliness I held within. I stared at the horrific scene in front me and felt downright calm.

I'd experienced the same calmness when Karen collapsed.

"Well isn't that sweet," Arrogance said. I imagined him jumping with glee and delight.

Arrogance, and the emotions I felt right now, frightened the bejesus out of me.

CHAPTER 5
SORROW ENDURES FOR THE NIGHT

Sirens broke the haze that held me, and the emergency medical technicians, firefighters, police, ambulance arrived. The medics worked on Alexis. Mark, Keith and a female police officer tried their best to calm down a hysterical Hannah.

A large crowd had gather outside by now. I always found it funny how I never saw these people on any given day, yet the moment something bad happened they had arrived in droves, ready to pass judgment before they'd learned the facts.

A female detective stepped to me and gently steered me toward the one of the squad cars. As we passed by the small crowd I heard their whispers.

"I can't believe she finally did. She'd finally killed that girl."

"Yeah I knew it wouldn't take long for her to snap. She's one of those loners you know. Got to be careful of them folks. They're all barmy!"

"Heard she stole the other girl's money and that's why they'd kicked her out the house."

"If that's true that's total shite. I hope they lock her up for good."

"Should've been locked up a long time ago. Bloody mental case!"

When we reached the squad car the detective opened the door and motioned for me to take a seat. She slid in beside me and signaled for her partner in the driver seat to go. The cruiser slowly maneuvered into traffic and headed south toward the precinct.

I gazed out the window, only half-aware of the world outside the claustrophobic comfort of the car. I shivered as I replayed the whole horrid scene over and over again in my mind as we drove through the city.

I had watched Alexis fly through the air like an ungraceful ballerina. I heard her desperate pleas for help; the sound of her body as it crashed to the floor; the snap of her neck and the crack of her bones as they shattered. I watched in silence as the blood poured out of her lifeless body.

"You okay?" the detective asked.

"Huh? Oh, yes. Thank you for asking," I replied.

She nodded but said nothing else on the way to the station. As we walked down the corridor, we passed all the usual suspects one would expect to find in a police station — drug addicts, slags and teenagers with bloody noses and scrapes from fighting. There were also a few well-to-do tossers, handcuffed and shouting about how they were gonna sue the pants of the cops.

"Stupid, bloody twats! Thought the rules don't apply to you, huh?"

Arrogance, this was so not the time.

I was escorted into an interview room at the end of the corridor. The room was small and square with four plastic chairs, a table and an empty water dispenser. There were no windows but there was a ceiling fan. The fan was set to high and circulated nothing but hot, muggy, humid air. The walls were grey and bare. The paint curled and falling from the walls. The fluorescent lights flickered and caused my head to hurt. The door behind me slammed closed with a loud bang.

I pulled out one of the chairs and sat down. I took a quick look around my surroundings and let out a sad sigh. My body sagged in the chair, and I laid my head on the table.

Not sure how long I was in there, but it felt like forever before the door opened and the female detective walked in. A male detective followed her.

The male detective had that *'why the bloody hell am I'm here and not in bed with my mistress'* scowl on his face. I guessed he was about fortyish. He was going bald and showed the signs of a growing beer gut. He also wore a suit that went out of style ten years ago, and his teeth were yellower than the sun at high noon.

The female detective was the complete opposite of her partner. She was in her late thirties and wore a stylish business pants suit with sensible but fashionable boots. She wore make-up, but unless you looked closely you wouldn't know it. She had the face of the teenager with only a few "wisdom lines," as my grandma called them, under her eyes.

Her eyes told me she'd had a long day, but the manner in which she spoke reminded me of those caring mothers in all those Lifetime Christmas movies I loved to watch. Her attitude said she understood what I had just experienced and wouldn't make it any harder.

Yet, as she read me my rights, her demeanor reminded me of the harsh realities of law. Her no-nonsense tone assured me she was not on my side, and she was not on Alexis or Hannah's side either. She was on the side of the law.

"Ms. Bailey, I'm Detective Chief Inspector Keri Chauncey and this is Detective Sergeant Hadeon Jaikan. We understand you've been through a lot tonight, but we have to get your statement, so please hang in there with us, okay?"

I nodded.

"Good," DCI Chauncey said. "You understand you're under caution correct?"

I nodded again. It seemed that was the only motion my body allowed me to make.

"Okay. Now please take us through the events of this evening. What happened?"

For the second time today I was explaining my involvement in a series of disastrous events.

***

An hour later, that wanker Jaikan told me I was free to go. He didn't seem very happy about it, though, and I could tell the words felt like ash in his mouth. Or was that the ash from his cigarettes?

I gathered my personal items and signed some forms before I headed toward the exit. And it was just my luck, or lack of it, that I'd bumped into Detective Inspector Harris, lollipop, crusty lips and all.

"Ms. Bailey, my, my, my. I heard about your flat mate's accident," he joked. "Two fatal incidents involving you in one day? That's a bloody con-winky-dink wouldn't you say, Eason? Guess we should get the Home Office to issue a public safety notice."

He looked me up and down, licked his lips, then shrugged and laughed. He glided like a snake down the corridor toward a group of prostitutes. They were waiting to be taken down to booking. Harris smiled gleefully as he chatted them up. I shook my head in disgust.

"Hope he's not asking them for the copper's discount," I said softly to myself.

"Don't worry," Eason whispered softly in my ear. "He's condescending and pompous but he's smarter than he looks."

His soft voice lit a fire inside me. I chuckled and turned to face him. He smiled. My heart skipped a beat and my body turned to jelly.

"Hello, detective. Nice smile. I ... I mean, nice suit," I stammered.

"Real smooth Karma," Arrogance chided.

"Heard about the incident at your flat. Are you okay?" Eason asked.

"A little unsettled but I'm okay."

"Are you sure? I know DCI Chauncey can be a hard-arse during interviews. Being a DCI, she mostly sits behind a desk doing administrative stuff. She loves it when she gets the chance to be a real copper again and not just a paper-pusher."

"On the contrary, she was quite respectful and understanding. It was that other detective, Jaikan, that was a nasty tosser."

He chuckled. "He is an arsehole."

We stood there in awkward silence for a few seconds. "Well, hum, I got some paperwork to finish up," he said.

"Right. I better get going. Gotta find a place to sleep tonight."

"Staying at friend's in the city?" he inquired. I'd almost forgotten he was a detective.

"You think they'd be safe with me," I joked. He didn't laughed. He just sort of stared at me like he couldn't believe I'd just said that. "Just a joke detective. I know, not funny." I grabbed my jacket and hurried toward the exit. Eason caught up to me. He gently grasped my forearm.

"If you need anything, please feel free to call." He handed me a card, smiled and then walked back down the corridor. I smiled, watching him go. Then I looked at the card I was clutching. It wasn't his business card.

It was a card for a free coffee at a local café, after the tenth purchase. And it only had four hole-punches. I sighed and exited the station.

The night air cocooned me in its protective folds, and I pulled my jacket tighter around me. Snow fell and quickly turned the city into a winter wonderland. For no other explanation other than a force of habit, I started toward Hannah's.

I'd just reached the entrance of a tube station when reality, along with a harsh blast of icy wind, smacked me in the face.

"Where the heck are you going, huh?"

For the first time tonight I actually answered Arrogance's question. I had no idea. Going back to Hannah's was not an option, and I doubted any of the other neighbors would let me stay in their flat. I had no friends or close co-workers who could put me up for the night. I checked my wallet. I had a few pounds on me, but not enough for a hotel. The ATM next too the tube station was broken, and the next closet ATM was five miles away.

The one credit card I had expired two months ago. The credit card company hadn't sent a replacement card. When I inquired as to why, the nice lady representative told me that after a review, my credit score was so low the company thought it was in the best interest of everyone to close my account. Another consequence of my parents' treachery.

I sighed, tucked my head into my chest and trekked on. My footfalls sank deeper into the soft snow as I made my way up the sidewalk. When I reached the entrance to the local park, I turned and looked back at the path I had left behind. The path was no longer covered in a crystallized, pure and beautiful snow.

No, the path was now nothing more than a pitiful mess of dark, murky, muddy sludge.

What an eerily symbolic representation of my life.

I couldn't go back to Hannah's place, not even to get my stuff. The police hadn't released the scene yet, though I'd be surprised if Hannah hadn't destroyed my belongings already.

The weekend was going to be long and harsh. I walked through the city until I came across a homeless shelter still serving food. After two hours of walking in the cold and wet snow I must've looked pitiful.

The sweet lady at the front desk took mercy on me. She didn't ask one question and simply handed me a blanket, a towel, a bag with some toiletries and pointed to the "Free Clothes" bin next to the lavatory. I grabbed a pair of skinny jeans, sneakers, socks and a long-sleeve Manchester United t-shirt out the bin. I sighed at the t-shirt.

Just what a lifelong Arsenal fan needed after the crappiest day of her life.

After I washed up and changed, I found the meal line. The only hot food that remained was the darkest green soup I'd ever seen. It looked like nasty baby food and smelt worse. It was served with a massive chunk of bread, the parts that weren't moldy was stale and dry.

Oh well, beggars can't be choosers, right? I sat at the table in the corner farthest from the crowd. Even after all I'd been through this evening I still performed my dining routine. I just finished saying grace when an older gentleman sat next to me. He was a tattered mess of ripped clothes and filth.

An oleaginous salt-and-pepper beard surrounded his portly face. His skin was buried under layers of dirt, and his hair was a nasty and tangled mess of grey curls with streaks of black. Except the smell, the man reminded me of Grandpa.

He smiled. Most of his teeth were gone and the few he had were rotten, and his gums were black and bleeding. I returned the smile then cautiously sipped my soup.

I gagged the moment the soup touched my tongue. My taste buds had never experienced anything so vile and disgusting. I coughed as the revolting mess slid down my throat. The gentleman chuckled softly then handed me a small cup of cream and cheese.

I poured a little cream into the soup and then mixed in some of the cheese. I took another sip. Yum! What a difference the cream and cheese made. I gulped down the concoction and used the mold-less parts of my bread to soak up what was left in the bowl.

The gentleman chuckled as he watched me down the soup

like it was my last meal.

"My apologies," I said. "That wasn't very lady-like."

"My wee lamb, you should never apologize for enjoying your food," he said in a thick Irish accent. I smiled and thanked him for sharing his cream and cheese.

"Name's Derrick." He wiped his hands with a napkin then stuck it out toward me. I took it and shook.

"Karma."

"Karma? What an interesting name. Well it's nice to meet you Karma. You with us for the evening?"

"Looks like I am."

"So glad to hear that. Me lads and I normally used the back storage closet. Security never checks it when they do their rounds."

"Uh-oh, what's this old geezer on about?"

"It's bloody dreadful out there, so I guessed you haven't scored many customers tonight huh? Well, me and my lads over there don't have much but a little is better than nothing, innit?"

He slid his chair closer to me and squeezed my knee.

"Customers?" Arrogance understood what Derrick was implying a split second before I did. *"What the heck? You gotta be kidding, right? This fool thinks you're a bloody slag. What a dumb prick."* Arrogance laughed and I shuddered.

"I'm sorry Derrick, but I think you got the wrong impression," I replied and tried to push his hand off my knee. "I'm not a slag."

"Sure you're not," he retorted with a giggle. He squeezed my knee a little harder this time. "C'mon wee lamb. We promise to be gentle." He moved his hand farther up my leg.

I pushed him hard and he fell out of his chair and onto the floor. The commotion attracted the attention of everyone in the dining hall. They turned and stared at us.

Derrick — a little shocked at being pushed — sat on the floor and snickered. A few seconds later, he got to his feet and picked up his soup bowl.

"Well, your loss. Barmy girl like you can't score much anyway. Should take what you can get." As he walked past, he purposely bumped the table and my milk spilt all over my clothes.

46

Derrick laughed and joined his lads at another table. He said something to them and then pointed at me. I imagined whatever he said had been hilarious, because they never stopped laughing — not even when they walked past my cot on their way to theirs.

"Just another sad bunch of horny and disgusting pensioners looking to get one last shag before they take the dirt nap," Arrogance chuckled.

I fought hard to control the tears that formed in my eyes. Even pathetic pensioners two steps from the grave found pleasure in teasing and tormenting me. I lay on my cot, covered my head with my blanket and cried myself to sleep.

Another atrocious payday Friday had finally come to an end.

CHAPTER 6
JOY COMETH IN THE MORNING

My head throbbed. It felt liked someone had tried to hammer a nail through a concrete wall. I sat up in my cot a little too quickly and that made my headache worse. I rubbed my temples in a vain attempt to ease the pain. The slivers of sunlight that slipped through the cracks in the window shade shined brightly light in my face. This only made my head hurt more.

"Are you okay?" a deep voice inquired. I opened my eyes slowly and focused on the mysterious voice. A man stood next to my cot with a worried look on his face.

"I'm sorry," I said. "What did you say?"

"I asked if you are you okay?" He knelt down on one knee and gazed into my eyes. His brown eyes scrutinized mine, likely looking for the cause of my momentary distress.

"Oh. Yes. Yes, I am. Thank you for asking," I replied. My stomach growled. We both glanced at my stomach for a second. The man chuckled.

"I believe that's your stomach's way of saying to get up now and get to the breakfast line before there's nothing left but day-old porridge and holiday fruitcake." I smiled while he chuckled and helped me to my feet.

The man who stood in front of me was tall and lanky. He wore old jeans and a collar shirt. I figured he must be one of the shelter's counselors. He had footballer's body and his voice was deep and full of bass.

His face said he was in his mid-thirties or early forties, but the way he wore his dirty blond hair slightly over his eyes told me he was trying to hard to relive his teenage years. On his right wrist was a cheap, child-like friendship bracelet. He wasn't handsome. The boyish look he tried to sport, along with his cheesy smile, would only charm women twice his age. We walked to the meal line where he handed me a tray and waited with me.

"Name's Rick," the man said. "I'm one of the shelter's counselors, and I run the job centre."

"Nice to meet you, Rick. I'm Karma."

"Nice to meet you, Karma."

I thought he would move on to another person, but he stuck to my side as the line moved forward. As I grabbed a fruit cup from the display cooler and waited for the line to move again, I noticed a surprised scowl on Rick's face. My overzealous imagination told me something was wrong with the fruit, so I placed it back into the cooler and grabbed a yogurt.

He saw my reaction, but didn't comment. Instead, he went into counselor mode and asked questions. "Angie, the lady who checked you in last night told me you had a bit of a rough night."

"Nothing too rough. Just a bunch of horny pensioners who got the wrong impression." I nodded toward Derrick and his mates. Rick smirked and shook his head.

"I'm sorry about that. I'm sure they were just joking and meant no harm. I'll inform Mr. Jameson, our director, about their actions. This isn't the first time I've heard about Derrick and his mates and their activities. Maybe Mr. Jameson needs to find them another shelter."

I shrugged and grabbed a travel-sized box of Special K cereal, two cartons of milk and a glass. I moved down the line and got a plate of eggs. I headed to the same table in the corner I sat at last night. Rick followed and sat with me.

"So, back to your rough —"

"Rick, I thank you for your concern but like I said nothing happened, and I'd just like to forget the whole scene." I waited for him to leave so I could begin my dining routine, but he didn't move.

"If you don't mind, I'd like to eat my breakfast before lunch is served," I smiled shyly.

"Go right ahead. We'll chat while you eat."

My anxiety flared up and my hands quivered. I closed my eyes tightly. I sat in the corner for a reason. I needed to perform my routine before I could eat. I'd never done it while someone was watching.

I opened my eyes. Rick still sat with his eyes boring down on me. I took a deep breath and exhaled slowly as I began my routine.

I unfolded my napkin and placed it on the right side of the table next to my eggs. I placed the fork and knife on the napkin. Then I salted my eggs. I grimaced immediately. I'd never salted my food without tasting it first.

I tried to continue my ritual, but the moment I struggled to open the box of Special K, things went awry. I pulled so hard on the package that when it tore open the flakes flew all over the table.

Rick chuckled. I frowned but tried to soldier on. When I spilt the milk as I poured it into the glass, I gave up and violently pushed my tray away. Rick's presence and constant glare unsettled me. I couldn't complete my routine. Without my routine I couldn't eat. I just couldn't do it. I hung my head and tried not to cry.

"Karma. It's okay," Rick soothed. "Although I must say I'd never seen a slag so flustered by my good looks. What do you say you and me spend a little time on my office sofa? Better yet, what about the storage room closet in back?"

Soft tears soon fell from my eyes. Rick let out a gut-busting belly-laugh.

"Such a sorry slag you must be. I bet even in your younger days you couldn't score more than £10 a night," he quipped.

He headed over to Derrick's table and sat with them. "Hey Dad you're right. That slut is pathetic," I heard Rick say. "No way she would score more than a few quid a night. Oh, gawd. Did you see that? I had her so captivated she couldn't even open a box of flakes."

Derrick, Rick and their crew laughed endlessly. I sat at the table and stared at my food.

"Pitiful Karma," Arrogance criticized. *"Pathetic, pitiful and just plain sad."*

Later that day, after I showered and replayed my pathetic breakfast moment, I borrowed a newspaper and looked for studio flats for rent. Despite the government deductions, and Mary's docking my pay every other week, I had managed to save a few pounds over the past two years.

I figured I had enough money for a security deposit and first-month's rent, even if it meant I would have to sleep on the floor and eat ramen noodles until I could afford a bed and simple furnishings. I was determined to find a new place to stay by the end of the day. By the time I walked out of the shelter, word had spread about my breakfast meltdown. I had become the new joke. There was no way I would return.

I had just stepped out the front entrance when I heard a man yell something. I couldn't make out what he'd said, but before I knew it, I was shoved face-down to the ground. I looked up just enough to catch a glimpse of men with semi-automatic rifles storming into the shelter.

A police officer again yelled for me to stay down and put my hands behind my head. It seemed like hours before I heard *'All Clear.'* A moment later an officer helped me to my feet.

"Miss, I'm PC Steves. May I have your name for the official report?"

I stared at him for a moment as I tried to gather my bearing.

"Miss, your name please?" PC Steves asked again.

"Oh, I'm sorry. Bailey, Karma Bailey." Steves chuckled slightly at my James Bond-type response.

"Now, Miss Bailey, how long have you been a resident of this shelter?"

DCI Chauncey's well-manicured hand tapped Steves' shoulder before I answered the question.

"I'll take it from here, Steves. Please gather statements from the other residents, then head back to the station and help Greg with the Intel on the suspects," she ordered. Steves nodded and headed inside.

"Karma, I'm surprised to find you here," she said. I stammered as I tried to explain my presence. DCI Chauncey held up her hand and smiled. "It's okay. It's just that after last night I thought you would be staying with friends."

"Uhm, no. I wanted to call but thought it best not to disturb them so late at night. I happened upon this shelter and stayed here."

"Why a shelter and not a hotel?" she asked.

"All the decent hotels in my price range were booked," I lied. DCI Chauncey cocked her eyebrow but said nothing and jotted down something in her notebook. Her expression told me she didn't believed one word.

"So this was your first time here at this shelter?" she asked. "Have you been to any others? For instance The Helping Hand or The Mission on Bread Street?"

Before I answered Derrick, Rick and the rest of their crew were marched past and toward the police patty-wagon. Even though they were handcuffed, they still resisted and tried to fight the cops. Rick saw me, and his eyes gave a *'you're dead'* gaze. He must've thought I was an informant — a plant by the cops to trap him and his crew.

"Karma? Karma? Tell me, have you ever been to those shelters?" DCI Chauncey asked.

"No. Never." As I answered her questions, I wondered why the cops were here. It had to have been something major because they don't call out the Armed Response Unit for just any regular bust.

"Hmm," DCI Chauncey said. "Have you had any interactions or dealing with Richard or Derrick Meade?

"No. I kinda met them last night. They thought I was a tart-for-hire and propositioned me for sex."

DCI Chauncey's eyebrow rose again as she scribbled more onto her pad.

"I told them I wasn't a slag, but they wouldn't believe me," I continued.

She had a worried expression etched on her face. "They didn't try to—?"

"No, no. They just called me names and made dumb jokes and the what-not. That's all."

DCI Chauncey let out a soft breath. "Did they say anything else?"

"They kept mentioning something about a storage closet in a

back room. Some room security never checked."

"Really? Hmm? Okay thank you for the information. Where were you headed when we arrived?" she asked.

I told her I was about to go hunting for a new flat. She nodded while writing again.

"I hope you find a nice place. And when you do, make sure you call me with the new address."

She read my puzzled expression and added, "You're still a person of interest in two separate investigations into fatal incidents, remember?"

I nodded. "Of course, ma'am."

"Take care," she said. She headed over and spoke with Steves for a moment. She pointed at something and he nodded. She patted him on the shoulder before she headed to her car and drove away. Steves came over a minute later and told me I was free to go. I grabbed my purse and headed toward the nearest bus stop.

***

I had found a few potential flats that, with a little tighter rein on my budget, I could just about afford. I narrowed it down to three flats. All contained a 'no flatmate clause," which was okay with me. After my experience with Hannah and Alexis, I thought it best to stay away from the flatmate option. Having a place of my own was worth me eating ramen noodles five nights a week.

Not counting going to work and occasional grocery shopping, I hardly ever ventured out into the city. However, winter was my favorite time of year and I always made an exception. The sudden drop in temperature, the rain, snow and the dark clouds that blocked the sun made others more despondent and pessimistic.

Despite the occasional winter wonderland effect that sprang up during Christmas season, winter was my favorite time of year because of the dreary weather. It was the one time of year the conditions seemed to match my lackluster and lifeless existence.

It sounded selfish, but it was the only time of the year I felt I wasn't alone in the world; that there were people out there like me who pummeled through the ice and slush, and wished they had enough money to say *'screw this crap, I'm staying home today.'*

I headed out to the first prospective flat, which was about a ninety-minute bus ride from the shelter.

To say my search started off on the right foot would be a complete lie. I fell asleep on the bus and missed my stop. By the time I caught a bus going in the opposite direction, I was two hours late and missed my appointment with the property manager. I called to reschedule, but the manager told me the flat had been rented and was no longer available.

"I see you're off to a great start," Arrogance grunted.

The second flat was about a forty-minute train ride to work. I stepped out from the tube station and looked around. My gut screamed for me to run away. The government had long ago forgotten this neighborhood. It was even passed over in the recent urban renewal plans that had been set in motion during preparations for the Olympics. Dilapidated buildings littered the area, and the flat was in one of them.

Anyone who could afford to move had fled this area a long time ago. The ones who stayed couldn't afford to buy milk, let alone move to a better and safer neighborhood.

The ramshackle building was covered with graffiti and anything broken likely stayed broken. The lift was out of order and the note from the city inspector indicated it had been out of service for some time. I stepped over a few drug addicts as I climbed the stairs to the manager's flat and knocked on the door and waited.

A moment later, an old man with a fringe of grey hair wrapped around his balding scalp opened the door. The dirty and stained overalls he wore barely covered his protruding stomach. He wore sandals with dirty black socks. His big toe stuck out from the hole in his left sock. He looked me up and down, then smirked.

"You the lady looking at the flat upstairs?" he asked. I'd simply nodded and did my best to hide the nausea that hit my stomach the moment I smelled his foul breath.

He handed me a key and pointed to up to a door. He told me to shout for him if I needed anything, then he slammed the door in my face.

I headed upstairs, unlocked the flat door and pushed. But it wouldn't budge. I used what little upper body strength I possessed to finally shove the door open. The moment I stepped inside I understood the reason the door had been so difficult.

I quickly covered my mouth and nose. The place was littered with liquor and beer bottles, very old Chinese food cartons and pizza boxes, with remnants of pizza still in them. It had likely been the perfect hangout for the homeless and drug addicts on this block.

The garbage stench hadn't been enough to overwhelm me on its own. But add in the vomit, boiled cabbage, burnt meat, unwashed clothes and mouse droppings, it came pretty darn close.

I stumbled through a mess of excrement, broken glass and chicken bones — at least I hoped those were chicken bones — to the kitchen. Then I checked out the kitchen and followed that with an inspection of the bathroom.

The loo festered in an acrid puddle of urine. The sink was covered in filth, hair and mouse droppings. The underside of the toilet seat was stained a nauseating dark brown, and the unmistakable aroma of human feces filled the windowless room.

Well, nothing a good washing up and loads of disinfected couldn't fix, right?

"Are you out of your freaking mind?" Arrogance questioned. *"Turn yourself around and get the heck outta here."*

I ignored Arrogance and opened my mouth to yell for the manager so I could tell him I decided to take the place.

Then in my peripheral vision, I saw something move in the corner. For a second I could've sworn it was a trick of the light. I quickly realized it was no magic trick.

A rat emerged from a hole in the wall and scurried toward one of the old pizza boxes. At this point in my life, one rat was not a good reason to pass on an affordable abode.

Then something happened that swiftly changed my perspective. One of my worst nightmares came to life right before my very eyes. From the corner where the first rat had emerged, another one appeared — and he did not come alone.

Rats! Hundreds, maybe thousands, of those buggers suddenly swarmed the place.

Okay maybe it wasn't a thousand rats, but a lot of those nasty vermin flowed from that hole like a gigantic brown wave. I was quickly surrounded by a tsunami of the vile rodents as they took over the entire place.

I received their message loud and clear — this was their home! I was the intruder, and I was not welcomed one bit.

I screamed and took off down the stairs. I don't believe I ever ran so fast in my life. I didn't have the luxury to be picky when it came to flats, but there are just some things not even I would ever live with.

Drug addicts, sex nymphs, bullying flat mates and touchy-feely neighbors were one thing, but a home filled with a legion of disgusting, disease-ridden, vile rats?

NO THANK YOU!

***

After the visit to the second flat, I had little faith the third one would be much better. I arrived twenty minutes early for my appointment. I used the extra time to walk around and get a feel for the neighborhood.

The area itself wasn't as bad as the previous two locations, but it wasn't Beverly Hills, either. Nevertheless, the flat was about a twenty-minute walk from city centre and was close to a tube station that would get me to work in about ten minutes. There were a few small grocery markets and a reasonably decent fitness centre down the block.

The building wasn't the dilapidated mess like flat option number two, but it could use a new paint job and some TLC in the garden areas.

The moment I walked through the front door was a moment I would remember for a lifetime. The saying 'never judge a book by its cover' must've originated here. I speculated the outside was a façade intended to hide the splendid wonders inside.

For inside this palatial bastion — the mixture of various modern and contemporary styles blended in blissful harmony with French Provincial and Tudor decor. The floor was tiled in fine marble, causing every step to echo off the beautiful walls. The chandelier presented kaleidoscopic hues that hypnotized anyone who dared stare at its wonders. Over-stuffed sofas offering the invitation to sit, put your feet up and take a load off surrounded the luxurious lobby.

A large flat-screen television was tuned to a classical music station, and it put me in a state of calm and relaxed euphoria. The concierge desk — yes, the concierge desk — was made of amber-colored wood and a grey granite top. Gorgeous paintings hung from the rich, cream-colored walls.

"Wow! Okay turn around and leave. There's no way you can afford a flat here." Arrogance said.

He was right, and I had turned to leave when a nice gentleman in his late fifties approached me.

"Good afternoon, Miss. My name is Eli, and you must be the young lady interested in the basement flat." I nodded and introduced myself. Eli shook my hand gently and escorted me to the level below.

I'd heard stories about people who knew their home was the perfect place for them the moment they'd stepped across the threshold. I experienced that same euphoria the moment I stepped through the doorway of that basement flat.

My potential new fortress of solitude was a one-bedroom, seven hundred and fifty square feet space of nirvana.

"Are you sure this is the flat mentioned in the advert?" I asked Eli. "It's not exactly what I pictured."

"You don't like," Eli replied. "Is there something specific you don't like? The color, the cabinets? I could ask Abe, one of our residents, to look into it. He's very handy."

"No, no. I love it. It's perfect."

"Yeah, too perfect. Something's strange here," Arrogances roared. *"No way this place should be available. There's got be extras and hidden fees that aren't in the advert. He's trying to hook you before he springs the extras on you after you sign the tenant agreement.*

"And the rent is exactly what was quoted in the advert. No hidden fees or extras," I asked Eli.

"No. The price quoted is exact. No extras. The flat is rent-controlled. This particular one uses far less energy, which helps keep your utility costs low. You're close to stores, schools — everywhere, really. It also has a private entrance, though we still maintain strict security protocols."

I walked through in utter amazement. The place had a rocky outcrop along one wall, giving it a rustic and rough feel, but it was warm and comforting with hardwood floors throughout the kitchen and living room.

The kitchen sported new appliances, and the bathroom had new fixtures and a garden-style whirlpool tub. There was a small office room next to the kitchen.

It was the bedroom that had sealed my decision. The room was a warm cream color, with tasteful gold trim. A beautiful mural that adorned one wall spoke to me. The vibrant scene depicted amazing waterfalls, beautiful gardens with blooming flowers, and groups of family and friends enjoying the day in heavenly surroundings.

The mural was amazing in its detail. However, I was drawn to the little girl who sat in the center of a hollowed out tree, far away from the joyous picnic. She seemed content with her spot but unhappy at the same time.

I saw myself as the little girl. She, like me, was happy and content being alone, but also unhappy at not being able to join in all the fun.

After I took a quick look at the spacious closet, I decided this was the place. It reminded me so much of my lost condo.

"Don't be stupid." Arrogance hardly ever stayed quiet for long. *"Something is not right."*

"Eli, I most certainly want the place, but I can't shake the feeling something's not right here."

"What do you mean, miss?"

"This place is gorgeous! You can get at least three or four times more than what you're advertising. It's too good to be true. Is there something I should know?"

Eli sighed and took a few deep breaths before he spoke. "This flat has been vacant for a long time because it was the site of a vicious triple homicide about six years ago. No matter how much we renovated and made it beautiful that little tidbit tends to either scare people away or attract the wrong crowd with their superstitions and all that other bizarre nonsense."

Hmm? Normally that tidbit would've scared me, too. Then again, I had no better options and doubted I would find something, anything, as beautiful as this flat in my price range.

"Well, Eli, I'd be lying if I said that doesn't frighten me a bit, but I doubt any otherworldly creatures are gonna waste their time on me. I'll take it."

Eli beamed and clapped his hands. I thought for a moment he would pull me into his arms and dance a salsa.

"Great. Look over the tenant agreement, while I run upstairs for a moment. I'll return in ten minutes. Is this okay?"

"Yes. Thank you."

"Good, good. I'll give you the grand tour when I get back. Is that okay?"

"Not a problem, Eli." He bounced back up the stairs. In the meantime, I toured my new flat in private and imagined how I would decorate each room. I almost had a gleeful moment.

As always the very moment I felt a nipple of happiness Arrogance was there with the bucket of cold water.

"How are you gonna decorate? You can barely pay the deposit and first month's rent. How are you gonna buy furniture, kitchen supplies, food? Oh my goodness. Talk about being way in over your head. This was not a good decision. You better tell him you changed your mind and head back to that shelter. So what if everyone there thinks you're a slag? You've been called worse, and by me, no less."

Eli returned with some additional paperwork and a spare key to the flat. He also had the security entrance card and code to my private entrance. I ignored Arrogance's tirade and signed the agreement. We then toured the building and Eli explained the various amenities.

Eli also explained the history of the building as we walked. There were originally five flats. About thirteen years ago the building's owner tried to sell it and the land to a development company, but all the tenants' agreements contained a rent-controlled clause.

The residents refused to leave. Since the owner couldn't increase the rent, he'd refused to make improvements on the building in an attempt to force the residents out. But the residents were tougher than the owner thought. They took the owner to court and won.

Eventually, the tenants bought the building and had owned it ever since. My basement flat wasn't part of the original five flats. It was a later addition, a renovation project by Eli and Ron, another resident.

I asked about the building's outward appearance and Eli laughed. He said the residents kept it that way as a form of protection.

"Which would you rather rob if you were a thief? A run-down building where the residents probably don't have many high-end items of value, or a building where you knew you could steal decent valuables to pawn?"

I thought about this for a moment. "The prison sentence is the same either way. So why not make it worth it? Going to jail for stealing a forty-year-old television that's not even cable-ready versus diamonds and jewels? Be hard to defend your reputation with the other inmates, I guess."

Eli laughed. "Hard to defend, indeed."

We toured the common areas, laundry facilities and game room. Eli explained the game room had been Ron's flat. In his will, he had requested his flat not be rented out, but converted to something the other residents could enjoy.

They decided to convert it into a game room, which could also be used for parties.

Eli and I were headed downstairs when we bumped into Lynn and Beth. They were sisters in their early sixties, and two of the original tenants. The sisters and Eli were the only remaining original tenants.

"Your highnesses," Eli greeted them with a bow. The ladies laughed and curtsied.

"Master Elijah how goes the day?" Beth asked in a voice spiced with royal charm.

"M'lady, the day goes ever so sweetly," Eli replied.

"My dear sir," Lynn interjected, "we seem to be experiencing some difficulties in our throne room. We'd be ever so grateful if you took a look at it."

"Madam, it would be my pleasure. As always, I am your humbled and loyal servant."

They all chuckled. Eli introduced me as the new tenant.

"Oh I'm so glad we finally found someone. Welcome to our

Shangri-La, my darling," Lynn said.

"Yes, welcome," Beth echoed. "When you're settled, we'll host a party for you."

"Oh, that's not necessary. Please, I don't want to be a bother. I'm not a party-person," I explained.

"Nonsense, Princess, they'll be a party in your honor," Beth rebuked.

"Yes, Princess, we'll hold a soiree the world hasn't seen since Her Majesty's coronation," Lynn added. "Ta-ta."

The ladies exited the building, walking arm-in-arm toward with party preparations adding exuberance to their steps.

Eli chuckled. "Those two are young at heart."

"Yes, they are. But I really don't want a party, Eli. I'm not very sociable."

"I feel miss, with the sisters, you'll have no choice. They've already anointed you a royal princess of the building."

"What if I don't want to be a royal princess of the building?"

He gave a great belly-laugh. "Afraid it's too late. You've signed the tenant agreement. If you will excuse me, Princess, I must attend to the highnesses' throne."

He bowed then headed toward the sisters' flat. His smile was wider than the English Channel, and he whistled a happy tune. I returned to my new flat and initiated my house routine.

When I'd moved in with Hannah and Alexis, I hadn't been able to do my routine. Not doing so of course caused me all sort of problems with balance and meditation. I closed the curtains, turned off all the lights and locked all the doors. Then I stood in the center of the room for exactly six minutes with my eyes closed — no more, no less — and just listened to the sounds of the Universe.

Afterwards, I would normally eat a sandwich. Since I didn't have any groceries, I sat in complete darkness for the next hour or two and listened to my rambling thoughts.

Had things begun to change for the better? After recent events was this a turning point? Weird, had I just experienced a spark of happiness for the first time in five years. Had sorrow for once in my life turned into joy?

Arrogance quickly answered. *"You can't be that stupid? Have you forgotten about Karen, Alexis and the police investigations? Your new 'fortress of solitude' won't protect you from that."*

As he often does, Arrogance extinguished my little spark of hope.

CHAPTER 7
DINING WITH THE SISTERS

I decided to grab a take-away for dinner and had just returned to my new flat. I also splurged a little and bought a sleeping bag from the charity shop down the block. The sleeping bag would be my bed until my savings recovered from the security deposit and first-month's rent.

Lynn and Beth trapped me in the foyer the second I walked in.

"Better start using that private entrance from now on, don't you think?" Arrogance suggested.

"Hello there, Princess," Lynn called.

"Whatchya got there?" Beth asked. After such a long and trying day I wasn't in the best mood for small talk. However, I didn't want to be rude to my new neighbors.

"Hello. Just getting ready to spend a nice evening in," I replied and held up my take-away. Beth frowned at the bag.

"Oh, Lynn, would you look at this? One of those dreadful supermarket-ready meals."

"Oh, no, Beth. We must not allow our princess to eat that. No, that just won't do."

"No, it won't," Beth agreed. "The princess must dine with us tonight."

"Yes, there is no other option," Lynn concurred. "Follow us, Princess. We'll have a nice and healthy supper ready in no time. Come on now. Chop-chop." She headed up the stairs, while Beth tugged on my arm and pulled me in that direction before I could flee to the safety of my own flat. She was surprisingly strong for a little-bitty senior citizen.

Their flat was not what I expected — a place liked my grandparents' in the country, with frilly decorations and furniture from the 1940s. But — as Eli had told me earlier — these sisters were young at heart. The flat was a very spacious three-bedroom and decorated in a textile house style with windows that allowed every iota of sunlight to illuminate the entire front room. The thick walls deafened city traffic noise, but every so often I heard the tell-tell siren of a police car or ambulance. The flat was a delicate blend of contemporary modernism, mixed with old-school charm.

"Princess, take your jacket off and relax," Lynn ordered. She hurried to the kitchen, while Beth headed to the bar in the corner of the living room.

"What's your pleasure, Princess?" she asked. "I bet you're a rum-and-coke girl."

"Ladies, I truly appreciate the gesture, but you shouldn't go through the trouble. I would feel much better if I headed down to my place and ate my take-away."

"Nonsense," they both sang in unison.

"Listen here, Princess, we know what it's like moving into a new place," Lynn shouted from the kitchen. "We're gonna make sure you have a good meal and built up those bones so you have enough strength to handle all that furniture you're gonna be moving."

"That's right," Beth added. "Now we can't help you move that stuff, but we're gonna do our part and put some muscle on these skinny bones."

She lifted my arm and wiggled it in the air. "My goodness, Princess when was the last time you had anything but a cracker? Lynn, we got our work cut out trying to put some meat on these bones. Looks like we're gonna have to stock up on roast for Sunday dinners."

Beth chuckled. I sighed. These ladies were not going to let me leave until after I had dinner. I felt the best thing to do was suck it up and get through the evening as quick as possible.

"In that case, Lynn, may I help you prepare dinner?"

"Why, Princess, thank you. No one has ever offered to help," Lynn replied and gave a polite sneer toward Beth. Beth snickered and took a sip of her rum and coke.

"Ha! No one ever offered because you always bite their heads off the moment they stepped anywhere near your *precious* kitchen," she barked.

"Don't listen to her, Princess. You come on in and stir the sauce," Lynn said. "As for you...." She pointed her wooden spoon in Beth's direction. "You shut your darn mouth, you old hag."

Beth shrugged and chuckled. She gave me a wink and gulped down the rest of her drink then fixed herself another. I felt she loved teasing Lynn, and Lynn loved teasing her back.

Lynn's kitchen had enough appliances to cater a small army. The color scheme was autumnal — the reddish-brown of the wooden floor stylish and complemented the brick walls.

The décor wasn't the only thing that had impressed me. The kitchen's pristine environment was more than a welcomed sight to my eyes. It was cleaned to the point of sterility. Every pot, pan, plate, cup, even tea towels, had its place and was neatly placed, stacked or hung. I relaxed a little more and went about helping Lynn with dinner.

Beth slouched into one of the over-sized recliners in the living room and watched some comedy show on their 42-inch flat screen telly. Lynn was a mad woman in the kitchen. She chopped vegetables, rolled dough, stirred sauces and tossed the salad. I did my best and tried to keep up. I felt I was more in her way than a helpful sous-chef.

An hour later, the food was ready and dining table set. We all prepared to dig into mushroom soup, bitter greens with tomatoes the size of peas, rare roast beef slices as thin as paper and fusilli in a pesto sauce. The rich aroma of the dishes was irresistible and lingered throughout the flat.

The small dining area was sophisticated in a discreet sort of way. The table was the centerpiece, but the area was surrounded by pictures of Lynn at various points in her life cooking in different kitchens.

A few photos were with celebrity chefs like Gordon Ramsay,

Wolfgang Puck, Robert Irvine, Jacques Pepin, Chan Yan-Tak and
— no it couldn't be — was that a picture of a twenty-year-old
Lynn with Julia Child? Now I knew why she was so good in the
kitchen.

As we sat at the table I slowly began my dining routine. The
ladies watched quietly. Like with Rick at the shelter, my hands
shook nervously, and I dropped my cutlery when I tried to place it
next to my plate. My anxiety flared up. Though I tried to keep it
under control, I couldn't stop the tear that fell from my eye.

I silently prayed for the strength to get through this without a
complete meltdown. What an embarrassment it would be to have
a mental breakdown in front of new neighbors.

"Oh, Lynn, you forgot the rolls again. Why do you always
forget the rolls? You got some unconscious hatred toward bread?"
Beth scolded and then scurried to the kitchen.

"Since you're in there, I forgot the butter, too," Beth shouted.
The loud clang of a tray being dropped echoed throughout the
dining room.

"Oh, I better go and check on her before she destroys my
kitchen," Lynn said. "Go right ahead, Princess, and tuck in. We'll
be right back." She strolled into the kitchen. I heard her and Beth
as they bickered back and forth.

I stared at the kitchen door for a moment then continued my
routine. The second I finished saying grace, the sisters popped
back in with rolls, jam and butter, and joined me at the table.

***

After dinner, I offered to help with the dishes, but Lynn
shooed me out of the kitchen. She and Beth both insisted I stay
for dessert. During dessert I learned more about their lives — the
places they've been; the men they've loved and lost; and how they
ended up in the 'Shangri-La,' their affectionate name for the
building.

"Tell me, Princess — what are your thoughts about Shangri-
La, so far," Beth asked.

"So far, so good. Not much to say, yet. I was a little unnerved
when Eli told me about the murder that happened in my flat. I
know it was six years or so ago, but its still somewhat unnerving."

The Sisters glanced at each other then broke out in gut-wrenching laughter.

"Excuse our bad manners, Princess. We must tell you that not one word of that story is true," Beth said.

"Not one bloody word," Lynn added. "It's just something we tell potentials to gauge their reaction.

"Yes. We've had a few scaredy-cats. The people who just couldn't live in a flat where a murder had occurred, no matter how long ago the incident happened," Beth said.

"Then of course, you have those really weird bloody twits who want to live there because *someone* had been murdered in the flat," Lynn said.

"Yeah. Going on about *dark energies* and *Hecate* and all that nonsense," Beth said. "Who wants to live with the shite? I sure as heck don't want to live in the same building with those creatures. There's enough weirdness out there. No need to invite it into your home, right Lynn?" They both laughed.

"But you, Princess. We knew you were okay before you had stepped through the entrance," Lynn said.

On my puzzled glance, Lynn explained that after I made the appointment to view the flat, Eli ran a simple background check. Nothing very detailed, just a check to see if I had a job and a steady income.

"No point in wasting time if you're just gonna turn out to be a deadbeat," Beth added.

"After your tour, Eli gave us a more detailed analysis of you," Lynn said and chuckled.

"Yes. He told us you were very upfront, honest and direct. He was happy you decided to take the flat, and so are we," Beth added.

"Now tell us, Princess — a nice girl like yourself no doubt has someone to help you move your stuff into your flat," Lynn inquired. I bet you have some strong, handsome Roman god to help you, don't ya?"

I choked on my soda. "Actually, I don't have any help. Fact is I don't have much stuff to move."

They both stared at me then glanced at each other, before their eyes set back on me. They waited patiently for me to continue.

"I'm a minimalist. A very simple life is all I can manage. You know work, home, fitness centre, repeat. I don't need much." The Sisters glanced at each then broke into a gut-busting laugh. They laughed so hard they cried.

"Well there it is, the laughter. The first of many to come," Arrogance chastised. He had managed to remain silent for the entire dinner. *"Took them a while but you knew sooner or later it would happen. At least they gave you a good meal first."*

I sighed and prepared to leave. "Thank you for the meal, ladies, but I think that's my cue to leave," I said. I stood up but Beth gently grasped my forearm and tugged me back into my seat.

"Sit down, Princess. Forgive us. We're not teasing you or making light of what you said," she apologized. "It's just that bit about being a minimalist, well, that's just —"

"Bloody shite," Lynn finished. She and Beth chuckled. "We like that sly sense of humor, but now out with it. You can cut the bullshit cause you are no match for us."

"Yeah, we're bullshitters from way-back," Beth said. They waited patiently for me to begin. They both actually looked interested and they seemed to care.

"Okay, where do I start?" I asked.

"The beginning is always good," Lynn encouraged.

So that's where I began. I told them everything about my parents, the HMRC, the government agents, and about being sacked from my high-salary job. I left out the bullying at my current place of employment. I also didn't tell them about Karen, Alexis or the police investigations.

"Well, well. I reckon the last few years have been very exciting for you," Beth said. "Wouldn't you agree, Lynn?"

"Exciting? Hell, I say the last few years have been bloody dreadful," Lynn replied. "I'm just amazed how you could go through all that and keep your social anxiety and OCD under control."

"I don't have OCD. I've just always done things, certain things, in a certain way because it makes more sense," I babbled on. Truth be told I babbled on like an idiot because Lynn's insight took me by surprise. Okay, so I had never *officially* been diagnosed with OCD, but even I couldn't kid myself.

Lynn caught my shocked expression because she chuckled and said, "Don't look scared, Princess. Beth and I know the signs very well. Have you not looked around our flat?"

I had and I noticed the kitchen wasn't the only pristine room. Nothing, absolutely nothing was outta place. Not even Beth's recliner. Everything was perfectly aligned or positioned very geometrically. The furniture wasn't feng shui but the overall designed was very relaxing and soothing.

"What's the deal, anyway," Arrogance barked. *"A couch is a couch; a chair is a chair. Who cares how it was positioned? You just sit on the thing. Feng shui! What a crock!"*

"Lynn has had OCD since she was a little girl," Beth explained. "Of course back in those days no one knew or understood anything about it, or even knew what to call it. Ma and Pa just thought Lynn loved to clean and organize, and they left her to it."

"It wasn't until I was forty-five and had a nervous breakdown in one of my restaurants that a doctor diagnosed me with OCD and adjustment disorder," Lynn said.

"She'd stabbed one of her kitchen commis after he put the apples in the same basket with the oranges," Beth jested. She and Lynn chuckled at the memory.

"Yeah, well, I should've sacked the fool long before that, and not cared that he was my boyfriend's nephew. He was as useless in the kitchen as his uncle was in the bedroom."

"Never mind that, we were just glad they decided not to press charges," Beth countered. We all chuckled.

"So, Princess, if I understand you have nothing at the moment?" Lynn questioned.

"Not exactly. I do have a set of clothes I got from the shelter and the suit I wore to work Friday and what I have on now. Oh, and the sleeping bag."

"But no furnishings?" asked Lynn.

"Uhm, no. I plan to use the sleeping bag until I can afford to get a bed."

"A sleeping bag? Oh no, that won't do. Will it Beth?"

"No, it won't. I'm calling Michael right now and getting him to open the shop." Beth pulled out her mobile and began to dial.

"Yes, call Michael. Tell him we'll be there in one hour," Lynn chimed in.

"Beth, Lynn, please don't. Don't call anyone. I appreciate you inviting me for dinner, but please, I can't accept anything else. I'm okay, really." The look on my face must have conveyed I meant what I said because Beth turned off her phone and Lynn slumped slightly in her chair.

"Okay, Princess, as you wish."

"Thank you. Now please excuse me, but I must call it a night and get some sleep. Thank you again for dinner."

Beth gave me a quick hug. She was a hugger, but Lynn knew better. She could tell being hugged was not something I enjoyed. She simply nodded as I made my exit.

I had reached my front door when a belated thought hit me. I had only known the Sisters for less than a day. Even in that short amount of time I learned they carried themselves with class, dignity and a strong sense of determination. They weren't the type to give up or compromise so easily. I wondered what would happen now. Would they tell Eli everything I told them? Would they work to get my tenancy agreement revoked? Would they gossip about me to the other residents?

"You know they will," Arrogance grunted. *"Old people, especially old tarts like them, love to gossip."*

CHAPTER 8
SUNDAY

I spent the night in my new flat and awoke relaxed and refreshed. It was the best night's sleep I'd had in six years. Even though I slept in a sleeping bag, I slept better than a baby. I showered, dressed and had just grabbed my jacket when the doorbell to my private entrance rang. I used the intercom to identify my visitor.

"Delivery," came a distorted male voice.

"Delivery? Sorry, you have the wrong flat."

"Is this flat six?"

"Yes."

"Is this Ms. Karma Bailey?" My over-cautiousness kicked in and I didn't respond. I hadn't been expecting a delivery and there was no way I was letting this guy into my flat. Plus, what company delivered on a Sunday?

"Look, is this Karma Bailey or not. I don't have all day."

I stayed silent. Eventually the guy returned to his truck and drove away. I waited ten minutes then headed out.

Eli was at the concierge desk when I returned from the grocery store two hours later. A young girl, about ten or eleven years old, sat next to him at the desk. She was hunched over a schoolbook.

"Hello, miss. Do you need some help with your groceries?"

"Oh, no, Eli. I can manage. Thank you."

"Of course, miss. Oh, excuse my poor manners. This is Ava,

one of our youngest residents. Ava, this is Ms. Bailey. Ava is Abe's daughter, and she's also my smartest assistant."

Ava looked up and smiled at me then went back to her book. I couldn't place it, but she reminded me of someone.

"Oh, miss, almost forgot. You had a delivery. I accepted it."

"You didn't let them into my flat," I asked, horrified that he had done so. "I wasn't expecting any deliveries."

"Oh no, no, miss," he reassured me. "No, the tenant agreement strictly forbids me entering your flat without your permission. I asked the men to leave the delivery in the hallway. I'll let Abe know you're home and have him help you move it in."

He took off before I had a chance to ask him what the delivery was. When I reached my front door, two very large boxes were leaned against the wall. The boxes contained a double-size bed frame, box springs and mattress. There were also a few small tote bags in front of a box containing sheets and a duvet. A note was attached to the box. I grabbed the note, thinking it was from the delivery guy.

"*Princess,*" the note began, "*I know you asked that we refrain from assisting you as you settle in, but as we told you, we know bloody bullshit when we hear it. Accept these small tokens as my way of saying 'Welcome to Shangri-La.' P.S. Michael said he'll have Georgina meet you at the shop at two this afternoon. Cheers, Beth.*"

Below was the address to a shop about thirty minutes away. I walked into my flat. Despite the nice gesture, I felt very ill-at-ease. This feeling gave Arrogance saw an opening and pranced upon my discomfort.

"*Of course you feel silly. Eventually, those two biddies are gonna ask you to do something for them. No one does anything out of the kindness of their hearts in today's world without wanting something in return. Well, except maybe you. And look where that got you.*"

I had just set my groceries on the kitchen counter when my doorbell rang. When I opened the door, I thought my heart was going to leap out my chest.

"Hello, Karma."

Standing at my door, wearing well-worn baggy jeans, a tight blue t-shirt that strained to cover his muscles, and deep-blue trainers was Detective Constable Alastair Eason.

He looked even more handsome than he did in his suit. Add in distinct cheekbones and angular jaw that currently displayed a cocky grin, he was deliciously gorgeous.

"Looks like we're neighbors," he said. I just stood there. The detective who was investigating my actions in a fatal incident lived in the same building. This can't be good.

"Way to state the obvious bird-brain," Arrogance chided. My heart skipped a few beats. It always did whenever I caught a glimpse of this man.

"Eli told me you needed some help with a delivery," Eason inquired.

"Wait a minute, you're Abe?" I asked.

He smiled. "Alastair Benjamin Eason. Abe for short."

"Oh," was all I could say.

"So, I'm guessing you don't want to leave this out here," he joked and pointed to the bed box.

"Yes. Oh, no. I mean, thank you. Do you need some help?" I stammered.

"No, I got it."

He struggled to lift the box. It was a bit heavy, so eventually he opened it and brought in the frame, piece by piece, and then dragged the mattress inside.

"I assume you want this in the bedroom?"

"Uhm, yes. Thank you."

He pushed the mattress into the bedroom and with as much grace as possible gently leaned it against the wall. I opened my mouth to thank him, but he returned with his toolbox. Apparently, he wasn't done.

"You don't have to do that," I said. "I can put it together."

"I know you can, but Eli and the Sisters would have my head if I let you, especially when they told me to put it together." I stood and watched as he went about his task. I knew I should put the groceries away but I had to watch him.

No, not because he was handsome or because his butt looked delicious in those jeans. No, I had to watch because I had no choice. I am extremely uncomfortable with people being in my home for more than the two minutes it took to deliver food.

It took him twenty minutes to put the bed together. I thanked him and expected him to leave. He didn't.

"Is there something else, Detective."

"Well the traditional neighborly thing to do after someone has helped you is offer them something to drink."

"Duh Karma," Arrogance chided.

"Right. Yes. Sorry. I only have water at the moment. Is that okay?"

"Water is perfect."

I headed to the kitchen, Abe followed. I grabbed a bottle of water from the grocery bag and handed it to him. "Sorry, it's not cold. I'd just returned from grocery store a few minutes before you arrived."

"No problem." He drank the whole bottle in one go. I stood there and watched his Adam's apple bob up and down. My goodness even his Adam's apple was beautiful.

"Get a grip on those hormones," Arrogance teased.

"Thank you," he said. I nodded. I expected him to leave then, but he hung around.

"Is there anything else, Detective?"

"Abe, please?"

"Is there something else, Abe?"

He stared at me in a way that made me uneasy. I began storing my groceries to escape his gaze. He chuckled at my box of ramen noodles, then tossed the water bottle in the recycle bin. I learned from the Sisters last night that Eli was big on recycling. He'd used his own money to purchase small recycling bins for every flat and the common areas.

"Nothing else. Just welcome to neighborhood." He left and I spent the next thirty minutes trying in vain to erase the naughty thoughts I had about how Abe looked without his clothes.

***

The doorbell rang about an hour later. My doorbell never rang this much at either of my other residences.

"Yes?" I said into the intercom.

"Ms. Bailey?"

"Who's asking?"

"My name is Phillip. I'm your chauffeur."

My chauffeur? "I'm sorry, Phillip, but I'm not sure what you're on about?

"My apologies miss. I was hired to drive you to the shop," Phillip politely replied. "Ms. Lynn said I was to drive you there, wait, then return you home."

I sighed. My two o'clock appointment. Those ladies.

"Sorry, Phillip. It's been a long day. Let me get my jacket, and I'll be right out." I grabbed my jacket, locked the door and met Phillip outside. The Sisters had arranged a high-class UberLUX for me.

"Hello, Phillip."

"Ms. Bailey."

Phillip was dressed in a typical chauffeur uniform — black suit, plain white-collared dress shirt, black tie with a diamond tiepin, black driving gloves, and shiny black wingtips. He stood next to a black Mercedes S600.

The car looked brand new and had not one scratch on it. Phillip tipped his driver's cap and opened the back passenger door for me. I took a moment and breathed in that new car smell before I slid in. Once I was seated, he handed me a note, tipped his cap again, then shut the door. Phillip started the car and safely pulled into traffic.

I read the note while Phillip navigated the city streets.

"Princess, when Beth told me about the bed, I knew I had to up her one. She has always been a sneaky little tart! Anyway, I've arranged a nice ride to the shop. Georgina will meet you, and she'll help you find the most extravagant attire. Can't have you wearing the same clothes day-in and day-out. Enjoy, Lynn. P.S. — Bet you didn't think this old tart knew about Uber, huh? LoL. Oh, and I know what LoL means, too."

I folded the note and stuffed it in my jacket pocket. I guessed the Sisters paid extra for the first-class treatment. I'd never used Uber, but I doubted their drivers wore driving caps or called themselves chauffeurs. When we reached the shop, Phillip opened the door and helped me out.

"Karma?" a young woman in her mid-twenties and dressed to the nines stepped toward me and shook my hand. "I'm Georgina. Nice to meet ya. Please follow me."

She walked into a shop called Michael's Boutique. I followed her inside and Phillip hung out at the car.

The word "boutique" was an inappropriate reference for this place. In fact it was downright insulting. The shop wasn't department store-large but it was a pretty decent size. I was in sensory overload as Georgina escorted me around. Everything I wanted and needed was here. I twirled around in jubilation. I always loved shopping, but hated crowds. The Internet and online shopping were magnificent innovations. I bought most of my stuff, including most of my groceries, with a click of my mouse. But every so often I braved the crowds and ventured into the stores.

Georgina smiled. "Well, Karma, you ready?" I nodded. Georgina and I spent the next three hours selecting clothes, shoes and accessories that were tasteful, but not priced to break the bank. We also selected various household items and nick-knacks.

I ultimately bought three decent columnist pantsuits — two in black and one in grey. I also found a nice pair of ankle boots, two pairs of black pumps, some trainers, a winter coat, four blouses, two pairs of designer jeans, and a cool lunch tote. The tote was a nicety but not a necessity. I just thought it was cute. My total was less than I thought. I still couldn't afford furniture, but it was nice to have a pot for cooking my ramen noodles. Georgina told me the Sisters had arranged for store credit for me, so I had time to pay off all the items I just purchased.

I thanked Georgina for everything. She and Phillip helped me load the packages into the car. Georgina informed me that she would arrange for the cookery items and other things to be delivered later in the week.

"Did you enjoy your time at the shop, miss?" Phillip asked.

"You know, Phillip, it wasn't bad. Not bad at all." He smiled and continued toward my flat.

No, today wasn't dreadful and miserable. We arrived back at the flat and Phillip carried my packages inside. He set them by my door but didn't enter my flat. The Sisters gave him instructions, and he followed them to a tee. I thanked him. I attempted to give him a tip, but he said it wasn't necessary, but to call him if I ever needed a ride anywhere. He tipped his hat and went on his way. I gathered my packages and went inside.

I woke up this morning, not happy, but not in a state of perpetual gloom, either. I had suffered and felt I had nothing left to give. But after today, I felt things in my life were finally beginning to get a wee bit better.

"Enjoy it while you can," the unbearable Arrogance grumbled. *"So, you got a nice flat, a bed and some clothes. That means nothing. Tomorrow's Monday, remember? Tomorrow you're back to being a lonely, bottom-feeder getting crapped on from on-high."*

CHAPTER 9
RESCUED

Monday morning I returned to work. Since I no longer had flatmates, there was no need to rush. I took my time and enjoyed a peace I hadn't felt since the day before Mum called and my world crashed down around me. I arrived at work early and sat at my desk with my eyes closed and embraced the morsel of serenity

I accepted the fact I was a strange person but the tranquility I experienced when thinking about Alexis and Karen made me sick to my stomach. Only murderers and people with no conscience actually took pleasure in other people's pain. I'm neither of those, so why did I have those emotions?

"Because you were happy," Arrogance answered. *"Admit it. You nearly squealed in delight because you knew they had finally gotten what they deserved for all their nastiness."*

The sound of Mary barreling toward my desk broke my contemplation, and I sat up straight at my desk. I'd thought she'd be out today mourning her *"friend"* Karen.

"Well, Ms. *Stank-Kay*, you got some nerve showing your face here after you killed Karen."

I remained silent and ignored her and simply proceeded to straighten the items on my desk like I did every day. My reaction irked Mary, because she scoffed, grabbed my chair and spun it so I'd face her. She leaned in so close to my face that I could smell the remains of her full English breakfast.

"Why are people so afraid of breath mints?" Arrogance quirked.

"Yeah just sit there and don't say a bloody word. It doesn't matter anyway, because I'm gonna make sure you get locked away for life." Fortunately Vince, one of the company's IT specialists, chose that time to make a surprise appearance.

"Excuse me, ladies, but I need to update some security software on this department's laptops."

Neither Mary nor I acknowledged what he said. Vince shrugged and went about his business. "Excuse me, Karma, but where's your laptop?" he asked.

Oh, bugger! I had forgotten the police still had it. They'd taken it as part of their investigation in Alexis's accident. Mary smiled when she saw my dismayed expression.

"Well, well, well. Ms. *Stank-Kay* has lost company property. I can't wait to report this to security and Employee Relations," she gloated and waddled her big hippopotamus-self back to her desk.

I watched while she picked up the phone and dialed. She smiled and laughed. I presumed the person on the other end of the call was Lily, Mary's friend from Employee Relations. They both were all too happy to ensure yet another demerit was placed in my personnel file.

"Sorry, Karma," Vince soothed. I had forgotten he was there.

"Not your fault, Vince." I slumped in my chair. No it wasn't Vince's fault at all. Heck, it wasn't even my fault. The fault lay entirely with Alexis and her spitefulness.

"Well," Arrogance gloated, *"looks like Alexis will get her revenge from beyond the grave."*

For the rest of the morning I sat at my desk while my paperwork piled higher and higher. I had no laptop to do the work so the papers just sat there. I did nothing but answer the phone and transfer calls. The clock on the wall ticked on, and I swore it sped up a few times — counting down to my inevitable doom.

Even when I was surrounded by people, I still felt so alone. I had felt like this every day I had worked there, but today was even worse.

After Mary's phone call, I felt as if the nuclear bomb that had hung over my head my entire adult life would drop at any moment. There was no fallout shelter, no doomsday sanctuary, no underground bunker.

No, there was nothing but darkness and gloom.

I'd just returned from the toilet when I saw Trent Steele. He was the Employee Relations director, Lily's boss. For him to visit our division in person meant I only had minutes before I'm tossed out on my behind. He stood in front of Mary's desk and every few seconds he turned and glanced at me.

His expression though hadn't given any inclination as to what he and Mary discussed.

Trent had only been with the company for eight months, but I'd convinced myself that was more than enough time to read my personnel file and join the '*how do we make life terrible for Karma*' club.

With my file, along with Mary's endless petulance toward me that seemed to seep from every pore of her huge body, Trent had more than enough to hand me my immediate termination notice. I groaned and sat down at my desk. Not long afterward Trent stopped by.

"Karma, I just spoke to Mary, and she told me about the laptop and some other recent issues. I have to say that I've also had my concerns about you. With everything that's happened —"

He paused and took a deep breath. I held my breath and just waited for the inevitable.

"Well, we think it's best if—"

"Here it comes! Told you so. You're about to be sacked. There goes your new flat," Arrogance said. As if I needed a reminder of the disaster that was about to occur.

"—we transferred you to another department," Trent finished.

"What?" Arrogance's shout nearly busted my eardrums.

"Really," I said. "Okay, what department?"

"Research and Analytics. I understand you have some experience in that field."

"Yes, I do. When do I report?"

"After lunch. The department manager, Christopher Russell, will give you more information."

"Yes, sir. Thank you."

"You understand this is just a trial basis?"

"Yes, sir. I understand. Thank you, again."

He nodded and headed back to the lift. I glanced at Mary.

I would've thought she'd be disappointed I hadn't been fired on the spot. But she wasn't.

She was fuming!

***

After lunch I reported to Research and Analytics. The department was located in the basement. Research and Analytics was the complete opposite to upstairs. The departments upstairs were designed with open floor plans, complete with floor-to-ceiling windows to allow as much natural light in as possible and painted in cheerful bright colors.

The walls in my new office were grey and there were no windows. But it did have more than adequate ventilation and lighting. The office was very quiet; the only sounds I heard were the computers and servers humming. Compared to upstairs, this place was cold and dreary.

How perfect!

I sat and waited in Mr. Russell's office. It was in a state of methodical clutter with a large grey-washed desk with three drawers on the right hand side was positioned at a right angle to the door. A cheap swivel chair, iMac, heaps of paperwork, spreadsheets and magazines, blue and black pens resided in a tin, while red pens were scattered over the spreadsheets.

Two floor-to-ceiling bookshelves, complete with alphabetized books arranged according to color, leaned against one another. Three, two-drawer filing cabinets with paper work stacked on top sat in the corner next to a plastic ficus and water dispenser with no cups.

Mr. Russell finally entered. I stood and shook his hand. He took a seat in his swivel chair and motioned for me to sit back down. After introductions, Mr. Russell gave me a brief overview of my duties, his expectations and a stern reminder that this was a trial run. Then he walked me through the department and introduced me to Julia and Tyson, the other two members. A company as successful as Vixen, one would have thought the Research and Analytics would've been a twenty-member team, but nope.

I was shown to my new desk. Mr. Russell plopped down a pile

of spreadsheets in front of me and told me to get to it because he wanted a summary report on the spreadsheets before close of business at five.

On my grey desk sat a desktop computer, a notepad, a stack of sticky notes, all in one color — blue. Two rows of bookshelves bursting from the seams with papers and spreadsheets sat in a corner.

Julia's desk was dead center and Tyson's was near the emergency exit. Like me, everything on his desk was positioned at least six inches from each other. Unlike me though, he had taped rulers to each corner of his desk — his way of ensuring everything stayed at least six inches apart.

Julia's desk was covered in spreadsheets, pens and magazines from various countries. They were all neatly organized on the left side. Carefully arranged on the right were her desktop computer, a leather notebook, and a framed photograph of a pre-teen boy.

After I had arranged the items on my desk so that they were the normal six inches apart, I got down to work. My new cubicle was located in the darkest corner of the room, which I preferred. Upstairs, the atmosphere was always filled with tension that had become so severe and pervasive that I could barely see more than a few feet in any direction. But down here I was able to relax, breathe and concentrate on work.

I smiled. Then I separated the spreadsheets and sorted them by date, then account number, then placed them in alphabetical order. A serene peace enveloped me as I worked. I found myself humming a holiday jingle in tune with the clicky-clack of my fingers as they danced across the keys. For the first time in five years my brain allowed me to enjoy what I was doing. I was able to focus and put all my energy into my task without worrying about the constant teasing, gossip, backstabbing, name-calling, or making those ridiculous coffee runs.

No longer distracted, I finished the research by two o'clock and emailed my summary report to Mr. Russell. It wasn't until four that he emailed a reply saying he would review the summary tomorrow.

I had finished my one and only project three hours before the deadline and now had nothing to do. I glanced at the clock for the one-millionth time. It was ten minutes after four. The rest of the room was quiet except for the clicky-clack of Tyson's keyboard and Julia's vigorous turning of pages as she reviewed magazine after magazine. Occasionally, she would jot something down in her notebook or quickly type something on her computer.

With nothing more to do, I searched and read about current news events on the Internet. I also took the time to sign up for a Facebook account, though I deleted the account thirty minutes later.

What was the point of having an account when you had no friends?

I was tempted to do a quick search on my parents, to see if there was any new information about them. But then I decided that with my luck the government still had me under surveillance. Instead of my parents, I searched for ramen noodle recipes.

I opened a drawer to pull out my notepad with my list of things to accomplish at home tonight, but I couldn't find it. I searched my other desk drawers, but the notepad wasn't in any of them. Realizing I probably left my notepad at my other desk, I took the lift up and found it there, all the while hoping no one would notice me.

I passed by the conference room and saw DI Harris and Detective Sergeant Jaikan seated at the table. Also at the table were Mary, Lily and Tasha. I saw Mary's expression change from tense to happy at something DI Harris said. She smiled as she rambled on. Jaikan laughed a few times as he wrote down every word Mary said.

I walked over to the door and tried to eavesdrop. I had just dropped to one knee and placed my ear to the door when Vince suddenly barreled down the corridor.

He hadn't seen me and tripped over me. The computer and other equipment he carried flew out of his arms and crashed to the ground with a loud boom. People came out of their offices; others poked their heads out from their cubicles to see what had happened. Not looking back, I sprinted to the stairwell before anyone saw me.

I raced down the stairs back to R&A. Taking a moment to catch my breath and drink some water I returned to my desk just as the phone shrilled very loudly. Julia and Tyson's heads shot up and they glared daggers at me. I mouthed "sorry," and lowered the volume.

"Research and Analytics, how can I help you?" I answered.

"You thought you were slick but I saw you."

It was Mary. She spoke in a low voice. I assumed she was at her desk and didn't want to be overheard.

"Thought you should know something, slag. The only reason Trent transferred you was because Jessica and the board wanted you out of the way while the cops interviewed everyone up here about you. And, yeah, I told them all about you. How you went on about Karen, me, Tasha, Lily and your flatmates and how you hated us and them. I even told them how you threatened Monica after you'd been caught taking credit for her work. Yeah, I told them every *bloody* word. Once the police are done here, so are you — you little bitch. Don't get too comfortable *Stank-Kay*. You're fucking history."

***

Mary's atrocious laugh lingered long after Mr. Russell told me to go home. On the walk I realized that without fail every time something relatively good happened to me, life gave me a swift kick in the butt, a subtle reminder that hope would always be fleeting.

I decided to walk home instead of taking the tube. The weather had reached that perfect winter mixture of snow, ice and frigid wind chill. What should've been a thirty-five minute walk took an hour. The weather and my own rambling thoughts had extended my trip. I wasn't able to shake off what Mary said.

Was it true?

I shouldn't have been surprised when Arrogance provided the answer.

"Of course it was true," he said. *"You know it's true. Why else would they transfer you to a new department? Think about it. They wanted you out of sight so the cops can do their thing. You hadn't actually believed what Trent said? Ha-ha. Trial basis? Get ready for a good smack in the face. Time to face facts, darling, and the facts say that it won't matter what the cops say, you're a dangerous liability for the company, now.* For once, Mary was right.

When the cops are done, so are you!"

I stopped at the intersection two blocks from my flat and waited for the light to change. The harsh weather was taken its toll on most of the city dwellers. In spite of the harshness of the season people still braved the situation in the spirit of holiday shopping. I watched as people walked with their heads down and moved at maximum speed. Their coats and scarves wrapped around them tightly and earmuffs snugged on their ears. Many people had ducked inside the shops simply to take advantage of a few minutes of warmth.

A man in a business suit and nice winter coat stood next to me at the intersection. He wore an earpiece and held a briefcase and his mobile in one hand. He shouted something to the person on the other end of the call, then furiously yanked out the earpiece.

"Damn assistant," he said to himself.

"Hard to find good help these days, innit?" I joked. He ignored me and focused on his text messages.

The light changed. The man glanced up quickly before he stepped into the street. He'd been so engrossed in his text messaging he didn't bother to look left or right before he stepped out. That meant he hadn't seen the sleek blue Mercedes that just ran the red light and now barreled toward him.

"Watch out," I shouted. I reached out and grabbed his arm and tugged him back to safety. I tugged so hard he lost one of his expensive wingtips and dropped his mobile. We collided and fell to the ground. Half a second later, the Mercedes sped past and utterly destroyed the shoe and the mobile.

"My phone! That's just great, just bloody great! I just got that phone. And do you know how much these shoes cost? Do you, huh?" he shouted at me.

"Sorry about the shoes and the mobile," I countered softly in an attempt to appease him. "At least you're not splattered over that guy's car."

"I guess not," was his quiet retort. "Damn, I'm going to be late now!" He quickly crossed the street and signaled for a taxi. I just saved his life and didn't even get a thank you.

"Are you expecting to get a medal, too?" Arrogance mocked. *"No*

wait, a knighthood from the Queen?"

I shrugged and continued home. I took small comfort in knowing the man at least looked both ways before he crossed the street to get the taxi.

Although I slipped a couple times on some ice, I made it home with no broken bones or scraps. I entered the building through the main entrance instead of my private one. Eli and Ava sat behind the concierge desk. Eli read the newspaper while Ava stared at the telly. Some mystery show was on.

I noticed Ava had a notepad in her hand and every few seconds she jotted something on the pad. I guessed the show wasn't mere entertainment for her, but more of a challenge. She looked determined to solve whatever the mystery was before the show's end.

"Welcome home, miss." Eli's energetic smile had quickly become one of the few things I looked forward to seeing every day. "Hope your day wasn't as dreadful as the weather?"

I smiled. "Eli, I wish I could say it wasn't, but alas, it was worse." I noticed I tended to speak in a slightly aristocratic tone whenever I greeted Eli or the Sisters. Their playfulness was rubbing off on me.

Ava hadn't noticed my presence, or she was too engrossed in her program to greet me. I nodded toward Ava. "Is she always so intense?"

"Not usually. It's that particular program. She and Abe always watch it together and try to solve the mystery."

"Oh," I said.

"Abe is working late tonight; something to do with idiots who use homeless shelters to run their drug and prostitution businesses. Can you believe that? Guess they figure it's the perfect setup — plenty of hopeless people looking for anything to ease their pain. I hope the cops lock them up for a long, long time."

So that was the reason DCI Chauncey had asked me those questions about the other shelters — and why she looked at me the way she did when I told her about how Derrick and Rick had thought I was a prostitute and propositioned me.

"People frustrate me sometimes," Eli said.

"Sometimes? Try every darn day," Arrogance countered. I agreed

with both their sentiments.

"Thank goodness the cops sniffed it out. Good night, Eli. Night, Ava."

Ava remained engrossed in the program, oblivious to Eli and I.

Eli chuckled. "Good night, miss."

CHAPTER 10
PARTNERSHIPS

The next morning I sat at my desk and twiddled my thumbs. I had nothing significant to do but stare at my computer screen. Mr. Russell hadn't given me another project to work on, or any feedback about the summary report I prepared yesterday.

Tyson sat at his desk with an angry scowl on his face. He was furious when I arrived this morning. Apparently, the cleaning crew moved the stuff on his desk last night. He'd spent close to two hours putting things back in order.

Evidently the cleaning crew did the same thing every time they cleaned the office. It wasn't because they needed to move the stuff to clean the desk. They did it as a joke and to mess with Tyson. Mr. Russell reported it to his superiors and explained why this needed to be addressed, but the company ignored the complaint and never took any action against the cleaning crew. I understood Tyson's frustration and anger. I brought him a coffee as a sympathetic gesture. He thanked me.

Julia focused on her work. She had spent the last hour on the phone with her son's school. I heard her say something about bullies, black eyes and a busted lip. I assumed her son was a recent victim of playground tyrants.

By ten o'clock, my morning coffee had gone cold. I poked at the dark surface and broke the congealing skin. The frigid dark liquid dripped and I ran finger around the rim of the mug. I know the premium beans had been wasted, along with the £6 pounds I paid for the coffee. An expensive treat that turned out not to be such a treat. I was bored, and watching coffee become sludge interested me more than watching the clock.

Mr. Russell finally called me into his office just before lunch.

"Karma, the summary report you prepared yesterday was —"

"Sloppy, inaccurate, worthless trash."

"Excellent and very impressive. It was extremely thorough and professional. And for you to get it done well before the deadline, well, that's just outstanding."

"Thank you, sir."

"I've just spoken with Mr. Trapper. He's the division manager for client services. Since you've shown you have more than the necessary aptitude for research projects, Mr. Trapper has agreed to let you work with a member of his team in researching and preparing a presentation for Jessica's pitch meeting with to the CEO of Torrance Clothiers in two weeks."

"Yes, sir. I appreciate the opportunity."

"Karma, remember, this account means a lot to Jessica and she wants everything to be spot on. So you can expect there'll be days where you'll have to come in early and stay late. You may even have to do work at home. Is that okay? Can you handle that?"

"Yes, Mr. Russell."

"Good. You'll be working with a, uhmm, hold on I got it here somewhere." He searched through the stack of papers on his until he found a sheet of paper. "Aww, here it is. You'll be working with a Monica Sander. Here's her number." I gingerly took the sheet of paper and left Mr. Russell's office. I almost vomited when I heard Monica's name.

Could this day get worse? My phone rang. I checked the caller ID. It read *Monica Sander*.

"Ask a stupid question," Arrogance teased.

"Hello Monica," I answered.

"Karma, buddy," she chirped. I could actually hear her fake smile. "Heard we're gonna be working together on client services department portion for the major Torrance Clothiers meeting. Well, thank goodness for that. I been a little nervous but now that

I know you're on the case, everything's all-good. Meet me at my desk in twenty minutes and we'll chat about the workload, 'kay. Thanks. Cheers."

I sighed and slumped in my chair. Julia glanced at me but said nothing and returned her attention to her computer screen. Twenty minutes later I ventured from the calm and peace of the basement to the appalling atmosphere of the client services department.

Tension permeated from every wall. Most of the associates were former stock brokers who had peaked and been "reassigned" from major stock firms. The department was responsible for scoping out potential clients and convincing those clients that Vixen Marketing could vastly increase their market share and profitability.

I was directed to Monica's desk. I'd expected to find her there reapplying her lipstick. A small blessing when I saw she wasn't. A box sat on her desk, with a note attached. I tore it from the box and read: *"Had a hot lunch date. Get started!"*

Arrogance screamed at me to leave the box, along with a note that said *"screw you, you disgusting slag."*

"Do it," he nagged. *"Go ahead. Whatchya got to lose, huh? They're gonna sack you soon, anyway."*

The workaholic in me overrode Arrogance. I sighed, grabbed the box and returned to R&A.

***

I worked late the next three days. What I couldn't finish at the office I brought home. I used my flat's private entrance and avoided Eli, the Sisters and the other residents. They were truly good and sweet people but I wasn't a social butterfly and would never be one. My job was in jeopardy, and I didn't have time to be neighborly.

I especially avoided Abe. Although tempted to ask him about the investigations, I knew he wouldn't give me anything more than the standard cop response. So I simply focused on work and the presentation.

Monica was no help whatsoever. She made sure she left me spreadsheets, notes and more unintelligible paperwork, but other than that — and a few stupid emails containing nothing but various emojis — she offered not one bit of help or feedback on the project. I would've had the research and presentation done by Friday morning if I hadn't had to spend most of my time deciphering Monica's incomprehensible notes and sloppy organization. It was like she never learned the English language.

"Why are you complaining, now? You've been doing that since the day you met the tart," Arrogance scolded.

Mr. Russell left me alone to work on the project unsupervised. I wondered why that was? Was he too busy with other projects? Or did he simply want plausible deniability if the presentation went pear-shaped? Anyway, I completed the research by Friday afternoon and began putting the presentation together.

I stopped by the market for groceries on my way home that evening and just reached my private entrance when Eli emerged carrying two large garbage bags to the bins. Saturday was our regular garbage pick-up day.

"Well hello there, miss," he called, that energetic smile putting me at ease. "Long time, no see. You aren't hiding from us, now, are you?"

"Tell him yes. Tell him it's because you all are a bunch of nosy busybodies," Arrogance pushed.

"No, Eli, not at all. I'm working on a major project at work and I've had to work late these past few days."

"You work too hard, miss."

I smiled. "Can't really call it work when you enjoy as much as I do."

"When you put it that way, I guess not. But since I've caught you, the Sisters are planning to host their annual New Year's Eve shindig. As a reigning princess of the building, we can expect your attendance, no?"

Party!

Just the mention of the word always sent chills down my spine. Parties were never something I enjoyed, and I had no intention of attending the Sisters' shindig.

"Eli, regrettably, I don't think I'll make it."

"Surely you can join us for a little bit. At least to help ring in the new year?"

"Thank you, but no. The project I'm working on is very important to the company. Please give the Sisters my apologies."

His shoulders slumped a bit, but he said he understood and would pass on my apologies to the Sisters. He dumped the garbage then went back inside. I was sorry, really sorry. Not about the party, but because my refusal seemed to ruined Eli's day. And there was no telling what the Sisters were going to say, or do, to me when they learned I would not be attending their party.

***

On Saturday I went for a morning run. Well, it was more walk than run. The ground was covered with newly fallen snow, but ice still lingered below. On my return, I decided to use the front entrance so I could say hello to Eli. I hoped he would brighten the day with one of his radiant smiles.

To my surprise, Eli wasn't at his usual spot behind the concierge desk. I guessed he was out on an errand.
Ava sat behind the desk. She had a huge textbook in front of her and was oblivious to everything around. I decided not to bother her and headed to the stairs that led down to my flat.

"Red, orange, yellow, green, green. Oh, shoot," Ava slammed her book shut.

"What's wrong?" I asked.

"Nothing."

"Really, you sure?"

She raised her head and looked at me. "It's just that I've been trying to remember the colors of the rainbow and what order they're in. I know red, orange and yellow and green, but after that I get all confused." Tears fell from her eyes. "I have a test on Monday."

"Hey, hey, none of that," I soothed. "If you dry your eyes, I'll give you the secret of how to remember the order." Ava sniffled and wiped her eyes with the back of her sleeve.

"That's better. Okay here's the secret. All you have to remember is the name Roy G Biv."

"Roy G Biv? Who is he?"

"What! You never heard about Roy G. Biv? He's only *the guy* who discovered the rainbow," I lied. "He named the colors after himself. Red, orange, yellow, green, blue, indigo, violet — Roy G. Biv. If you remember his name you'll never forget the colors of the rainbow."

Ava's face lit up and she smiled for the first time since I walked in. "Roy G. Biv, really?"

I smiled. "Really. Whenever you get stuck, just say that name and the answer will come to you. Okay?"

"Wow. I wonder why my dad didn't tell me about Roy G. Biv," Ava said. "He's a police detective and he's really smart. Well, he's smart when it comes to cop stuff but not so much on school stuff," she chuckled.

I smiled as Ava repeated the mnemonic device. "Good, you got it. Just remember Roy G. Biv," I encouraged.

She was still repeating the mnemonic device when I headed to the laundry room later that afternoon. She smiled and waved when she saw me. Sometimes I got a warm feeling when I helped another human being. I felt rewarded somehow.

"Yeah, right. Helping people sucked. Just give them time. Sooner or later they'll turn on you."

Arrogance never missed an opportunity to snuff out any warm feeling I had.

***

My rough draft of the presentation was ready by Wednesday afternoon. Mr. Russell reviewed the presentation and praised my efforts. He then offered a few tips on polishing the presentation.

"So how has it been working with client services?" he asked. "Any problems?"

I wasn't sure how to answer. Was this my boss checking on my welfare or a thinly veiled probe to see if I would gossip about other departments?

"No problems, sir. Everything is going smoothly."

Mr. Russell nodded but said nothing else. For the rest of the day I worked on the presentation and incorporated many of Mr. Russell's suggestions. By the end of the day I was satisfied with the presentation.

Monica had not returned any of my calls or emails, but I wasn't surprised when she called just as I was about to upload the presentation to the company's shared server for the A/V guys to pull tomorrow.

"Karma, where's the presentation? Is it ready?" she barked. "My boss has been bugging me all week about it. Apparently Jessica wants to do a dry-run tomorrow to work out the kinks before Friday's big presentation. Did you know about the dry-run?"

Mr. Russell had mentioned the dry-run. Since Torrance Clothing was a big player in the retail and online shopping arena, it would be a major coup for Vixen to steal their £200 million account from their current PR firm, Carter Marketing and Public Relations. And it wasn't just about the money, either.

Acquiring the Torrance's account would not only establish Vixen as the number one PR firm in the country, but it gave Jessica another opportunity to stick it to Carter. What better way to do that than steal away Carter's first, and most loyal, client?

"Yes, Monica. I was just about to upload the presentation to the servers so the A/V guys will have it for tomorrow."

"Good, good. Let me know when it's uploaded so I can tell my boss."

"She means let her know so she can tell her boss she did all the work." Arrogance said.

Once the presentation was uploaded I emailed Monica and let her know. She emailed back a smiley face emoji.

Arrogance pushed for me to reply with a vomit emoji. I didn't.

***

The dry run went smoothly, or so I hoped. I didn't attend. Mr. Russell had signed Tyson and I up for a two-day teambuilding seminar. This was senior management's latest initiative to help increase morale and productivity.

Every department had to pony up two people. Since most of the managers and department heads were attending the dry-run, they signed up their low-level employees and interns for the seminar, instead.

The teambuilding event was a dismal bore from the start. The facilitators and guest speakers were tedious and the presentations were mind-numbing twaddle, and this was only the first day. If I heard one more person blurt out *"teamwork makes dream work a reality"* once more, I was going to cut out that person's tongue.

"Oh, please. You would do nothing but crawl under your desk and hide." Arrogance teased.

The first day of the seminar ended at two, so I returned to my desk. I found that Monica had emailed me. In fact she sent ten emails and called ten times in the span of two hours. I just opened the first email when my phone rang.

"Where the hell were you? Why didn't you respond to my emails?" It was Monica. I heard the panicky tone in her voice.

"Monica, I just got back from the mandatory teambuilding seminar. I'm reading the emails, now."

"Well, hurry the fuck up. My boss is all up in my arse."

"Not literally I hope." I chuckled softly at Arrogance's joke. I read the emails. Monica had sent a list of things Jessica wanted changed in the presentation. I read over the list. Simple changes, nothing major.

"I got the list. Doesn't look too complicated. I'll have it done before I leave tonight."

"You're a lifesaver. When you're done just upload to our department shared account. My boss said he wants to do one last review. Don't worry, I'll make sure it gets to the A/V guys in time for the meeting. Oh and you don't have to attend the meeting. My boss said he'll handle everything."

"Sure Monica."

"You know why they don't want you there, don't you? It's so they get all the credit and you get the shaft again."

The changes took me two hours to make, and I uploaded the presentation to client services department's shared account. Monica replied with another silly happy-faced emoji.

At five I grabbed my things and headed home. On my way to the tube station I caught a glimpse of Monica and Sergeant Jaikan seated at a coffee shop across the street. My first thought was that Jaikan was questioning Monica about me. I ducked into the nearest store and watched their conversation for a few minutes. The longer I watched, the more stressed and worried I became.

"May I help you, miss?" a store sales associate asked.

"No, thank you, just looking."

The sales associate scoffed and returned to her spot behind the counter. I would be mad to if I thought people were just ducking in my store to get warm and not to buy anything.

I returned my attention to Monica and Jaikan. I had just made a mental note to forgo my inhibitions and ask Abe about the investigation when I saw Monica shove her tongue down Jaikan's throat. He responded just as eagerly. He grabbed and squeezed her butt and she rubbed her hands up and down his groin. Their gross public display sickened me to my stomach.

"You're just jealous," Arrogance teased. *"Admit it."* I shook Arrogance's words from my head. I exited the store and continued to tube station.

CHAPTER 11
DARKNESS DESCENDS

I have lived total acceptance that my life wasn't the stuff of Disney fairy tales. That no matter what I did my life would always end, not happily ever after with my Prince Charming, but in a flaming mountain of dog poop.

So, I didn't noticed anything out of the ordinary as Tyson and I made our way back to our office in the basement after the teambuilding seminar ended at lunchtime.

Today was Friday, the day of the big presentation with Torrance Clothiers. Everyone, except the Research and Analytics department, were on edge. It's wasn't every day the company had the chance to snag a £200 million account away from a competitor.

As Tyson and I walked down the corridor toward the lifts, people stopped what they were doing and stared at me. Their looks ranged from disbelief to shock to anger. Since people tended to look at me this way every day, I paid it no mind.

That is until I passed by Mary, Lily and Tasha. They stood at Mary's desk, and the moment I passed them, their faces lit up brighter than fireworks on bonfire night. Their smiles were filled with a cold malicious delight that no one would mistake as any form of genuine affection. Their expression stayed with me the entire ride down to the basement.

Mr. Russell was in my face the moment Tyson and I stepped off the lift. He was livid.

"Karma, what the hell is wrong with you? Jessica is furious and raining down fire and brimstone. My office — *Now!*" he roared and stormed into his office and waited for me to enter. I didn't have the faintest clue as to what he was on about, but I guessed the Torrance Clothiers presentation didn't go well.

I glanced at Tyson, who shrugged, then to Julia, who simply shook her head. I headed into Mr. Russell's office. He slammed the door with such force the walls shook.

"Karma, I'm giving you one chance to explain to me what the fuck is wrong with you? Jessica just ripped me a new arsehole and I'm close to being thrown out on that new arse." His whole body shook so violently I thought he was in the midst of a massive coronary.

"Mr. Russell, I don't understand what you're talking about. Did the presentation not go well?"

He let out a forced laugh. "Not go well? It went well, all right, given the fact our boss was humiliated in front of her peers and employees, and the company just lost a £200 million account. Yes, I would say the presentation went *bloody well!*"

He collapsed in his chair and let out a frustrated sigh. "Why'd you do it Karma? Was it just some sick revenge thing or something?"

I still had no idea what he was talking about. "Mr. Russell, sir, I'm not sure as to what you're referring to."

"I'm referring to you adding video of our boss's executive assistant in the midst of a sexual orgy with Torrance Clothiers CEO's *FIFTEEN-YEAR-OLD SON!*"

Oh, holy Jesus! The room went quiet. Not even the crickets chirped.

"Mr. Russell I don't know what happened, but I assure you I did not do that," I said.

"Karma, save it. Monica Sander and Mr. Trapper have already explained how you were the last person to make any changes to the presentation."

"Mr. Russell, I did not do that."

"So you can deny you made changes and uploaded a new version of the presentation at four-fifteen yesterday?"

"No you can't deny it." Arrogance answered.

"No, but I was told the changes were based on feedback given by Ms. Paterson during the dry-run. Monica Sander sent me the list of changes."

Mr. Russell shook his head. "Karma, Jessica didn't request any changes."

"Shut the front door! You are screwed."

"Believe me. I can show you the emails Monica sent me."

Mr. Russell let out another frustrated sigh. "Since I knew you understood this position was given to you on a temporary basis, I wanted to give you the benefit of doubt."

I sent up a silent prayer of thanks.

"So I asked IT to perform a check on your profile and all incoming and outgoing emails." He handed me a printout from IT.

"As you can see, IT found no incoming or outgoing emails from Ms. Sanders. In fact, aside from an email sent on the day I assigned you to the project, where she asked you to meet her later that day, you and her never worked together or communicated anything about the presentation. Ms. Sander also explained you never returned any of her calls in reference to the project. In fact, here's a copy of the email you sent her and told her that her help wasn't necessary. You also, accidentally I presume, courtesy copied Mr. Trapper on that email as well. Given the amount of emails he receives each day, he didn't have the chance to read that particular one until after today's incident."

All kinds of thoughts flashed inside my head. I tried to slow them down so I could breathe normally, but I couldn't. My breaths came out in wheezes and words deserted me. I sat there, head hung low, totally defeated.

"Mr. Russell, please believe me. I had nothing to do with what happened during the presentation," I pleaded. Tears fell unrestrained from my eyes.

"I'm sorry, Karma. My hands are tied. You've become too much of a liability for the company. This was the last straw. Gather your things and wait at your desk until security arrives to escort you from the building. You're fired!"

I felt sick. My heart hammered in my chest. The room spun so fast and so much that I had to clasp my hand over my mouth to keep the vomit from spewing. My lungs strained to inflate and provide air to my body. I wanted to run but my legs were paralyzed and I couldn't move.

Not even Arrogance offered any quip retorts or snappy comebacks. He went strangely quiet. My brain spun faster than a merry-go-round. Emotions — fear, anger, disgust, hate, sadness — all attacked at once, and I had no defense with which to fight back.

Then the world went black.

***

A bright light shined in my face. I held my hand in front of my face and tried to block the intrusion but the light kept coming back. I blinked three or four times in a row before my eyes finally adjusted to my surroundings.

"She's okay," a strong and deep male voice said. "No signs of a head injury or anything serious." I looked up and saw a medic kneeling over me. The events from earlier flooded my mind, and I remember why I now laid on the floor.

"Mr. Russell if you just sign here, we'll be on our way," said a female voice. I couldn't see her but I had heard the irritation in her voice.

The male medic helped me sit up. He checked me once more then he helped me to my feet. He steadied me when my legs wobbled and I nearly collapsed again. He asked if I was okay and I slowly nodded.

Mr. Russell handed the forms back to the female medic but remained behind his desk. He thanked her for their quick response. The female medic smirked and then gathered their medic kits. She watched as the male medic helped me to my desk. He handed me a cup of water and asked me again if I was okay. I nodded and sipped the water.

"Perfect," the female medic said. "If you experience any pain, nausea, or dizziness go to the nearest A&E. Let's go, Larry."

She turned and stormed toward the lifts. I wasn't sure what crawled up in her butt and died. She seemed annoyed at treating a female patient who fainted. Maybe Mr. Russell's explanation of why I fainted offended her. To her, I must be just another weak woman who couldn't hack it and pulled a fainting spell to garner extra sympathy.

Larry, the male medic, gave me a quick smile before he dashed to the lifts and caught up with his colleague.

Mr. Russell walked over to my desk. His eyes were red, puffy and filled with sorrow. His body language told me he hadn't believed a word of Monica's story. He also knew that it didn't matter how much he defended me, once the IT report validated Monica's story, the company went into damage control mode.

I had been labeled a liability long before this incident and the company wasted no time in terminating my employment. Mr. Russell was only the reluctant messenger.

"I'm truly sorry, Karma. I really am. I wish there was something I —"

Two security personnel, a male and female, arrived, and he never finished. He shook his head and, with shoulders slumped, slowly walked back into his office and softly shut the door.

Tyson and Julia had said nothing throughout the whole ordeal. They glanced at me with sadness in their eyes then returned their attention to their work.

"Ms. Bailey, we're here to escort you from the building," said the female guard.

"I understand. May I have a few minutes to pack up my things?" I asked.

"Yes, ma'am," the female guard replied. They waited patiently while I packed my things into a cardboard box. I grabbed the box and security slowly escorted me toward the lifts. I gave a small smile as I passed Julia. There were tears in her eyes, and she looked as if she wanted to say something but the words failed her.

As I passed Tyson's desk, he glanced at me, then gently nudged his handcrafted penholder an inch to the left so that it was no longer exactly six inches away from the edge. A tear slowly fell from my eye. Tyson's small gesture said more than words ever could.

In our very short time together, Tyson, Julia and I had become, well, we weren't quite friends. We were more silent colleagues who understood and respected each other's unique quirks. We each had been humiliated or bullied by others in the company. That pain we'd suffered bonded us in a way words never could.

While security and I waited for the lift's arrival, I glanced around the office one last time. Vixen Marketing hadn't been the ideal workplace for me but it had been a job when I needed one, and I had tried to do my best every day.

However, as it had always been since primary school, life gave me a quick reminder that my best simply wasn't good enough.

***

I've experienced many embarrassments in my life, including the nightmare of urinating on myself during my A-levels, but I never experienced being drummed out of an office building.

People lined the corridors on both sides like they were watching a parade. If I hadn't known better, I would've strutted down the hall like some American naval officer who was retiring after years of honorable service and walking the hall one final time.

But this was no friendly farewell. There was no applause; no well wishes; no hugs or kisses. There were tears, but those were only mine. As I was escorted down the corridor, people shook their heads in disbelief. Others sneered and reigned in their urge to spit on me. A few people simply refused to make eye contact and stared at their shoes.

To them I was the antichrist. I was the person who just cost the company £200 million and at the same time just screwed their chances of receiving a major end-of-year bonus.

I saw Mary and Lily as I passed by my old section. There they stood with gigantic smiles on the faces. Mary had a particular *"I told you so"* gleam in her eyes.

Monica and Mr. Trapper were there, too. Mr. Trapper stood, arms folded across his chest, with a disgusted and angry sneer etched across his face. I guessed he was there to ensure I was tossed out on my butt. Monica leaned against a wall and pretended not to care. But as I walked past, I saw that evil smile of hers.

As I trudged along, Lily *accidentally* knock the box out of my arms. One final torment for the road.

"Oops," she chirped. "So sorry." She and Mary let out gut-busting laughter. Security stood there, but other than the warning stare the female guard gave Lily, neither guard moved an inch. I bent down and picked up the items that had fallen out the box. I replaced the cover and stood up. Security continued their task of marching me out of the area and toward the entrance.

When we reached the front the female security guard relieved me of my security badge and handed me my official termination paperwork.

My head hung down as it had most days when I left work. This time was different, though. This time, my head hung low not because of the sadness and heartache I normally felt after a day of being teased, tormented and bullied. Today my head hung low because, well actually, I wasn't quite sure why.

Maybe it was because, even though I had been tormented since day one, I had come to accept torment as a fundamental part of my life. Being teased and bullied had become such a part of my daily routine I had come to depend on it; that somehow I needed it to get through the day. Now, I didn't even have that.

I headed down the street toward the tube station I normally took home. During the walk, I formulated the following plan:

1. Lock myself in my flat
2. Avoid all human contact
3. Cry for a few days
4. Search the Internet for jobs at the local fast-food restaurant

I'd just reached the tube station when suddenly behind me came the unmistakable blare of a police sirens. A police vehicle skidded to a stop near the curb, tailed by two other cop cars. All had flashing blue lights whirling in circles. The officers jumped from the vehicles and stood next to the doors.

I, like everyone else, froze where I stood and wondered what happened to warrant such a response. Had a criminal escaped the police's clutches and jetted down into the tube station? Had there been a fire or some other emergency? Like everyone else, I stared at the uniformed officers and waited for them to give further instructions. Were we to use another tube stations? Were the tube stations closed and we had to use the buses? The officers focused on crowd control or exhibited a heighten sense of urgency. What was going on?

Then I saw Detective Sergeant Jaikan. He'd approached me with a smile on his face and a subtle spring in his steps.

"Ms. Bailey, I'm here to arrest you. You do not have to say anything. But it may harm your defense if you do not mention when questioned something which you later rely on in court. Anything you do say may be given in evidence. Do you understand?"

I said nothing. I just stared at Jaikan. I couldn't comprehend his words. All I knew was a uniform male officer had cautiously removed the box I carried from my arms then a female officer handcuffed me.

"If you would be so kind—" Jaikan said. He stretched out his arm and indicated I should head toward the police vehicle near the curb.

I was shepherded to their cruiser. I thought being sacked and thrown out the building had achieved the title of my most embarrassing moment. Then it dawned on me — being arrested and thrown into a police vehicle in front of a thousand commuters, tourists and city dwellers was definitely more humiliating.

Since I held a box in my arms, and was about to enter a tube station with said box moments before police suddenly appeared on scene, I imagined the thoughts running through people's minds as they watched the female officer push me into the back seat of the police vehicle.

"Another filthy terrorist. Thank God the cops got her."

"What the hell? If you hate it here so much, fucking leave?"

"Wonder what excuse some fucking deadbeat defense solicitor is gonna draw up? 'She was an abused wife who didn't know better?' No, wait, 'she was abandoned by her parents?' Or 'she was just dumped by her boyfriend and wasn't in her right frame of mind.' What a load of twat. I say toss her wanna-be terrorist arse in a cell and throw away the key."

"She's not really hot, but I'd do her. Of course, only in some dark alley where no one could see me. But still, I'd do her."

The female cop slid into the back seat beside me. Jaikan hopped in the front, while the male officer slid into the driver seat. The sirens blared as the car jetted into traffic and toward the station.

Everyone remained silent during the ride. I stared out the window the entire way, but every few seconds, I looked toward the front and caught Jaikan's sinister smile in the rearview mirror. At one time he blew me a kiss.

Of everything that happened to me today — that was the sickest.

***

When we arrived at the station, I was escorted into the same interview room I'd been in following the incident with Alexis. A female uniformed officer stood at the door.

Thirty minutes later, Jaikan and another female detective entered the room. The female detective nodded to the uniformed officer. I'd half-heartedly expected to see DCI Chauncey and not a new detective. Jaikan and the detective sat at the table opposite me.

"Miss Bailey, I'm Detective Sergeant Kissme. Detective Sergeant Jaikan and I have a few questions in reference to a current investigation into a fatal —"

"Kiss-me? Really? With a name like Kiss-me you don't have to wonder how she made it up the ranks."

I guessed the cat hadn't quite cut out Arrogance's tongue.

"Detective, I'm still not quite sure why I'm here? I told DCI Chauncey everything about the incident with my former flatmates. Surely she'd verified everything I said in my statement?"

I glanced at Jaikan. He smiled and took out a tin of tobacco. He pulled out a huge clod of snuff and stuffed it into his mouth. He chewed over and over again on the cricket-ball size wad in his cheek. He smiled so wide I could see his disgusting and rotten yellow teeth. My stomach rolled as I fought off the urge to vomit.

"I'm sorry, Miss Bailey but I'm not referring to that case. I referring to your involvement in the suicide of Mr. Stephen Charles Quinn," DS Kissme clarified.

"Who the heck is he?" Arrogance questioned.

"Stephen Charles Quinn? I don't know that person. I've never heard that name," I said.

"Miss Bailey, please. Now is not the time to play dumb. Tell us the truth and maybe the prosecutor will go easy on you," Kissme countered.

"I assure you, Detective, I don't know this person. I've never met him in any capacity," I replied. At that point Jaikan slammed his hands on the table so hard and fierce, the whole thing shook. His action scared me. It apparently surprised Kissme, too.

"Stop with the dumb and innocent routine, lady," he shouted. "We have evidence of your complete involvement. Now tell us the truth before I toss your worthless arse in a cell."

"I'm not acting. I have no idea what you are talking about or what incident you are accusing me of being involved in," I retorted. Jaikan's face turned bright red and he looked as if he would jump across the table and beat me to a bloody pulp.

"Miss Bailey, Mr. Quinn committed suicide after a video was posted online of him having, uhmm, relations with a certain Mr. Peter Franks. I assumed you know Mr. Franks?"

I nodded my head slowly.

"And can it be assumed you are aware of the video of which I speak?" she asked.

I nodded my head again.

"We have evidence that shows the video was posted online using a Vixen computer system. We checked their servers and traced the IP address. It led back to your department. A more thorough search showed that the video was posted from your computer — using your login credentials — at four-fifteen yesterday. The video was set to post at precisely nine this morning. By ten, the video had gone viral and at noon Mr. Quinn leapt to his death from the roof of his school."

"He's dead because of your actions," Jaikan yelled. "You're gonna pay for that."

I sat in stunned silence.

"Miss Bailey, as you can see this is a very serious charge. The courts are getting more and more harsh about these types of crimes. Mr. Quinn may have gone off that roof, but as far as the courts are concerned, you pushed him, and that's murder."

I stared at her. Detective Kissme softly took my hands in hers. "This is your only chance to help yourself," she said softly. "Tell us the truth. Tell us why you did it."

I shook my head. "Detective, I swear I played no part in this. I only heard about the video when my boss, Mr. Russell, told me about it. Honestly. I had nothing to do with the video. I haven't seen it, for goodness sakes."

Kissme released my hands and sat back in her chair. She crossed her arms over her chest and stared at me. I could tell she was trying to decide if I was telling the true or was just a very good liar.

"Save the bullshit!" Jaikan yelled at me. "We've caught you with your damn fingers in the tin."

I jerked upright, panicked and frighten by Jaikan's tone. I slid my chair farther away from the table, in an attempt to put distance between him and me. He stalked over and stood next to my chair. He bent down and his bloodshot eyes glared at me.

"It's over. You're done," he growled.

"No, no, no," I cried. "I played no part in this. I am not the reason that young man harmed himself. You're wrong. You're wrong. I want to go home. Please, I just want to go home."

Jaikan scuffed and began to pace the room. "Go home? Go home? Tell you what you little bitch —"

He spat the huge chunk of tobacco at me. The disgusting mess hit the side of my face. I sat there stunned as sickening residue ran down my cheek. He rushed toward me, but before he could grab hold of me Kissme and the other uniformed officer grabbed him and held him back.

"Sergeant, that's enough," Kissme yelled. "That's enough!" Jaikan settled down, but his eyes still shot daggers at me.

"You need to go outside and calm down," Kissme suggested. "Go smoke a cigarette or something."

"Yeah. I need a cigarette," Jaikan scoffed. He pointed at me. "I'm sick of dealing with liars and sad fucks like you." Jaikan stormed out.

Kissme waited a moment before she returned her attention to me. She handed me a napkin before she retook her seat. I wiped the disgusting mess from my cheek, fighting the urge to vomit as I did.

"Detective, what the hell is going on in here? I could hear the commotion all the way down the hall."

The familiar voice of DCI Chauncey brought some small relief to my beaten and battered psyche. Sergeant Kissme didn't answer Chauncey's question. She slowly clasped her hands and stared at table.

"Detective, I asked you a question and I want an answer," Chauncey commanded. Kissme lifted her head slowly and proceeded to explain how she and Jaikan were in the midst of interrogating a suspect in the Quinn case when Jaikan went off-script. Kissme nodded toward me in the corner.

"Oh, bloody hell! Why wasn't I informed Ms. Bailey was a person of interest in the Quinn case?"

Kissme explained that Jaikan had gotten information from his confidential informant that I was about to skip town. Jaikan said there wasn't time to inform Chauncey, they had to move fast and make the arrest now.

Chauncey listened, but I could tell she was seething at the lack of protocol.

"Detective, I want a word with you and Jai—"

"*Medic!*" someone yelled. "We need a medic over here." A loud commotion sprung up in the corridor, interrupting Chauncey. She rushed out and Kissme followed, but not before she instructed the female officer to stay with me. The officer nodded but didn't shut the door.

From where I sat I saw two police officers trying to talk to Jaikan. He tried to explain what was wrong, but he couldn't. His breaths came out in ragged, shallow gasps.

Then he doubled over and began choking. His head hung low toward his knees. His left hand grabbed one of the officer's shirts and clutched tightly. His right hand held one of those roll-your-own cigarettes.

When Jaikan's eyes caught mine, he glanced from me to the cigarette, then back at me. He smirked and shook his head.

His face — the same face that looked upon me with repulsion the second he met me — now exposed his inner feelings. His face said he knew death was about to claim his soul and these were his final moments on earth. Instead of sorrow, sadness or regret, he cracked a weird smile, displaying those rotten, yellow teeth in all their glory.

The cigarette fell from his hand and he crashed — face-first — onto the concrete floor. One of the officers rolled Jaikan onto his back and began CPR.

"He's not breathing and I'm not getting a pulse," the officer yelled. Another officer grabbed an automated external defibrillator. He tore opened Jaikan's shirt and attached the AED pads.

"Stand clear," he yelled. Everyone back away. The officer pushed the button and it delivered a shock to Jaikan's heart. Jaikan's body jerked violently. A few seconds passed before the first officer began CPR again. Jaikan still hadn't responded. They tried another shock but got the same result. They continued CPR until the medics arrived a few seconds later and took over.

Another two minutes passed before they had Jaikan on the gurney and were rolling him out of the building.

Chauncey and Kissme waited a moment after Jaikan had been taken away. Chauncey then turned to Kissme and spoke softly to her. Chauncey's words, though delivered as a whispered, must've hit a sore spot. Kissme nodded slowly. Chauncey glanced at me once more before she walked away.

Kissme returned to the interview room but she didn't sit down. Instead she stood and hung her head. A few moments later she spoke, but so softly I barely heard her.

"Miss Bailey, on behalf of the department, I sincerely apologize for the inconvenience we've caused you. I've been informed the information we received, which subsequently led to your arrest, was not entirely accurate or credible. You are no longer a person of interest in this case and you're free to go."

She glared at me for a few seconds. "Please assist Miss Bailey in retrieving her personal items and call her a cab," Kissme instructed the female officer at the door. The officer nodded and Kissme hightailed it down the corridor and out of sight.

"Ma'am, if you would follow me, please," the officer said.

I wanted to go home so badly but I couldn't move my limbs. My mind and body were too beaten down. I was totally exhausted after everything that had happened today—being sacked, escorted out the office building, arrested in the middle of a major city centre and accused of murder.

But all I could think about now was why had Kissme told me I was free to go? What had Chauncey told her? Was this all a trap? Would some government agent arrest me the moment I stepped outside?

"Stop with the boo-hooing and get up? I want to go home," Arrogance ordered.

The officer sensed my dilemma. She came over and helped me to my feet before she calmly led me out of the interview room.

CHAPTER 12
HOPE SOARS

I hid safely in my flat during the next two weeks. Out of sight, out of mind. None of the other residents checked on me or knocked on my door, which many of them had done since I moved in. I figured Eli told them about the major project at work and how important it was. They probably figured I used my private entrance to come and go.

But I hadn't stepped one foot outside my flat at all. I simply sat in total blackness and sobbed. By now I lost all will to live. I mean what was the point?

No matter how much I thought I had succeeded, reality was always right there to knock me to the ground. I had been humiliated and sacked from my job; arrested and accused of murder. I had no income, no job prospects, no references and no friends.

On top of everything, I received a letter from yet another debt collector. I apparently owed £8,000 for damage to a hotel penthouse suite. A belated Christmas present from Mum and Dad, thanks.

Would I ever experience true happiness in my life? My life would only get worse, right?

Silence.

Even Arrogance had abandoned me. My constant companion ever since that little creep Tim Foster first teased me in grade school when I was five had finally deserted me. If even Arrogance couldn't handle the weight of everything that had happened, was there any hope for me?

So I made a decision. Today I would venture outside, get some fresh air and a new perspective. I used my private entrance and avoided the lobby. I returned about an hour later and bumped into Eli as he emerged from the front entrance.

"Aw, miss, there you are," he said. "We've been worried about you. You were locked up in your flat for so long, the Sisters were two minutes away from calling in a search and rescue team. Shall I tell them you're okay?" He chuckled. I made an attempt at a smile.

"Please do so. I just have a lot of work to finish."

"So will your work be completed in time for you to attend the party?"

"No, Eli I don't think so. I have too much to get done."

"Oh c'mon miss?"

"Sorry Eli, I just can't."

"Surely you could join us for just a —"

"FOR CHRIST'S SAKE, WILL YOU STOP BADGERING ME? I SAID I'M NOT COMING TO THE STUPID PARTY."

I shouted so loud, and with such force, my body shook and I dropped the prescription bottle I carried.

My outburst startled Eli. It shocked me.

"Eli, please, please forgive me. I'm so sorry I shouted at you," I begged.

He smiled, but it wasn't his usual sweet smile. He said nothing as he bent down and picked up my prescription bottle.

"No, miss, please forgive me," he said and handed me the bottle. "You have enough on your plate. I should not have bothered you." He walked back inside.

Eli had been so sweet and understanding ever since I moved in, and I repay him by shouting and losing my temper. The shame of my outburst added to my disheartened soul. The floodgates opened and tears fell uncontrollably.

I was now convinced the decision I made earlier was the correct one.

***

I was lying on my couch when my doorbell rang later that evening. I checked the keyhole and saw Abe standing there. He smiled as I opened the door.

"How can I help you, Detective?"

"It's been a while since I've seen you and I wanted to stop by to pass on my thanks for the help you gave Ava. She got the highest score on the test and the teacher praised her for being the only student in her class to know the colors of the rainbow in order."

"Tell her I said good job," I said weakly and tried to shut the door. My mind and body were not in the mood for company and I tried to end this visit quickly. Abe placed his hand on the door and gently pushed it wider.

"There's another reason I stopped by; a more serious, police reason. It's regarding our investigations into the incidents involving your co-worker and your flatmate. I need to clear up a few things. May I come in?"

I reluctantly stepped to the side and allowed him in, then shut the door. Abe carried with him a soft-covered briefcase. He sat down on the couch and placed the briefcase on the coffee table. He motioned for me to have a seat on the couch. He pulled his notepad from the briefcase, flipped a few pages and found what he needed. He gave me his oh-so-serious detective face, which is not what I needed to see at the moment.

"Ms. Bailey, I just need to ask you again if you intentionally tried to harm Ms. Greene or Ms. Young."

Dejected and miserable, I answered the question with the same answer I had already given a hundred times.

"No, Detective I did not intentionally try to harm Ms. Greene or Ms. Young. As I said multiple times before, I did not harm them in any way. I did not provide aid due to the momentary shock I experienced when the accidents occurred."

"Well, thank you for your time and your assistance. Our investigations determined that the incidents were indeed accidents, and no charges will be filed. The investigations are officially closed."

"Thank you. Now, if that is all, I'm really tired and I want to go to bed."

Abe stood and walked to the door. I followed. His hand was on the doorknob when he suddenly stopped. He turned and faced me.

"I understand, Ms. Bailey. I do have just one more question."

"Yes, Detective?"

"How many of these did you take?" he asked and picked up the empty prescription bottle I left on the entryway table next to the door. His face registered a mixture of disappointment, hurt and anger. I stared angrily back. I felt rage boiling inside.

"Why the heck does he look so crossed? Who the heck does he think he is? What gives him the right to judge?"

Arrogance returned with a vengeance and every inch of me wanted to give in and let him take complete control. I had been teased, betrayed, bullied, humiliated, sacked and arrested. I was now blacklisted in the corporate world, and not even the McDonald's down the street would hire me.

I wanted to explode! I wanted to shout! I wanted to throw a temper-tantrum and bang my hands on the ground like a baby! I wanted to vent! I wanted to curse the world and send it to the deepest, darkest pits in Hell! If there was ever a time to let Arrogance out in full force, now was it.

But the instant I looked at Abe's face, I saw genuine concern in those piercing blue eyes. Those eyes smashed what was left of my heart to pieces and crippled my resolve. My knees buckled and my head, which was now too heavy to hold up, slumped into Abe's chest. The dam of tears broke and I sobbed uncontrollably.

Abe put his arms around me and held me tightly. "It's okay. Everything will be okay. We'll get through this, I promise."

***

After I'd calmed down, I spent the next hour unburdening myself to Abe. I told him about everything — my social anxiety disorder; my undiagnosed OCD; my parents' legal troubles; the HMRC and the near-bankruptcy; the book club; Hannah and Alexis and how they treated me; how I was treated at work. I even told him about the episode at the homeless shelter.

"Whew," he said. "Well that's a shit-ton of shit," he said. "You've been through a lot —"

"That's not all," I interrupted. "I was sacked last Friday. On top of that, your pal Jaikan arrested me right in the middle of the city centre. "

He let out a long breath and nodded. "DCI Chauncey told me all about that at Jaikan's funeral."

I stared at him.

"The tobacco he used to make his cigarettes had some kind of bacteria that got mixed in during processing. The company issued a recall on that brand about a month ago, but looks like Jaikan didn't realize he had one of the tainted tins. Kissme told me he never smoked that brand before either, so guessed that's why he didn't know about the recall."

"Whoa," was all I could say.

"Professional Standards were already in the midst of a thorough review all the cases he handled or were involved in. All Chauncey would say is that if Jaikan hadn't died on the job, he would've been thrown in jail for the rest of his life."

"Wow," I said. It was the only word I could think of that summed up the Jaikan debacle.

"Oh, I almost forgot. I have something to return to you," Abe said. He leaned over and opened the flap of the briefcase he had brought with him. He pulled out my company laptop and handed to me.

"The department thanks you for your cooperation and apologizes for any inconvenience and any ill-treatment you experienced."

I ran my hand over the laptop. Just seeing it again brought back painful memories of that fateful day. I sniffled and wiped away a few tears.

"I guess you won't be needing that anymore," Abe said. I turned and glared at him. He chuckled and shrugged his shoulder. "Well, you won't."

We both laughed. It was the first time I laughed in a long while. Once our laughter died down, Abe returned to serious detective mode.

"Listen" He held up the bottle. "I know getting sacked and arrested may have seemed like the last straw, but committing suicide is never the solution to any problem."

I stared at him in astonishment. "Suicide? What are you talking about? I wasn't about to commit suicide."

"Really?" he asked with a hint of sarcasm.

"Yes, really. Those are my iron pills. I took the last few just before you knocked on my door."

He studied the prescription label, then shook his head and laughed.

"Eli."

"Eli? What does Eli have to do with anything?"

"He told me and the Sisters what happened earlier today. He said you didn't look okay and had a large bottle of pills. They were worried you'd do something regrettable."

"And they asked you to check on me?"

"Blackmailed me, actually."

"Blackmailed?"

"Yes, blackmail. Lynn threatened not to make her famous six-layered chocolate crunch cake for the New Year's Eve party tomorrow."

I stared at him, puzzled, unable to believe what he was saying.

"What? It's bloody delicious. The woman knows how to bake, and I'm a sucker for chocolate cake." We both laughed.

"Are you okay? Seriously, no joking?" he asked.

The look of concern on his face was heartfelt, not simply a by-product of his detective training. He deserved the truth. He'd listened to my whole story and hadn't judge or offered anything but a kind ear.

"Go ahead, tell him the truth," Arrogance dared. *"Go right ahead. After they've locked you up in the mental ward, don't come crawling back to me."*

"Yes, I am," I answered. "Things aren't pretty right now, but committing suicide was never in the plans. I just needed some alone time to figure things out. Have a good cry, that's all. Please feel free to let the others know I'm okay."

"Why don't you tell them yourself? Come to the party tomorrow. Everyone wants you there—Ava, the Sisters, Eli—"

"You?" I silently prayed.

"Everyone. Besides, you are the reigning princess. Tradition decrees you must attend."

"I need to think about it. Is that okay?"

Abe nodded. "Okay. Party begins at eight."

"Thank you for checking on me," I said.

"Anytime," he gently grasped my hand and kissed it. "Your highness."

I closed the door and went to my bathroom. After washing my face, I stared at my reflection in the mirror. I opened the medicine cabinet and grabbed the bottle of sleeping pills I picked up earlier today.

I stared at the white pills and thought how much they would ease my pain. Tears ran down my recently washed face.

Arrogance — ever my constant companion — was right there. Instead of the surly and tough character he'd always been, he now spoke with a much more tender and caring tone.

"It's okay. It was just a little white lie. Abe wouldn't have understood. No one would ever understand. They would have just locked you away. Out of sight, out of mind. You'd be just another mental case, just another government statistic. You want to feel peace and serenity, right? Just pop a few pills, have a glass of water, then go to bed. I promise everything will be all right tomorrow. You will feel no more pain, no more hurt. There'll be no more teasing, no more bullying, no more worrying about if people like you or not. Everything will be okay, and you'll have everlasting peace with people who truly love you."

I stared at the pills in my hand. Then I stared at myself in the mirror. Arrogance was right. The pills would make all my hurt go away.

"Will they?" came a voice I had never heard before. *"Before you pop these pills, answer this question, 'when has Arrogance ever been nice to you?'"*

Common Sense had arrived, just in the nick time. Had she been with me all along, just waiting in the wings until I truly needed her help?

I tossed the pills and the bottle into the trash.

CHAPTER 13
HAPPY NEW YEAR

New Year's Eve.

Large snowflakes fell and covered the land in crystal elegance. If the angels in Heaven had a pillow fight, this is would resemble the result. Crisp, white, pristine snow truly transformed the city into the winter wonderland I only read about in stories.

I spent most of the day agonizing about whether to go to the party or not. Abe's visit, and the touching way he left, played with my heart. However, my social anxiety played with my head.

"Do whatever you want to do." Common Sense was fast becoming my new best friend.

Eli, the Sisters, Ava and everyone had treated me with nothing but kindness and respect. They deserved the same in return. I felt I could keep my fears in check for a couple of hours.

So at five minutes past eight, I took a deep breath, exhaled and then headed to the party room and faced my fears.

***

The music was loud but not so thunderous that it made the tables shake. Vegas-themed neon lights flashed everywhere. There were about twenty-five people in the room and another twelve on the roof. People danced, laughed, ate, joked and just had a good time.

The DJ was hip and on fire, and the bartender served the

cocktails with a smile and a dose of cheer. There was even a balloon artist and a magician to entertain the children.

But, there was no denying the food was the true reason people were here. Lynn had done a glorious job. Tables strategically placed through the room were loaded down with delicacies.

Every holiday food I could think of, and some I never knew existed, waited to tease the taste buds. Sweet fruit and salty nuts, cheeses, breads, vegetables, sweets, and deli meats complemented the delicious delights.

Lynn's six-layered chocolate crunch cake had a table all to itself. Good thing I don't count calories, because I don't think I could count that high.

The cake was layer after layer of crazy rich, decadent, beautiful, delectable scrumptiousness. It was a stunning picture of chocolaty goodness — a magnificent display of the chef's culinary talents. I now understood why Abe didn't want to tick Lynn off. A chocolate cake of this magnitude was a perfect way to ring in the New Year.

I surveyed the room from the corner. I'd faced my fear of attending the party but my social anxiety kept me from interacting.

"Glad you made it," a deep voice whispered in my ear. It was a voice I recognized instantly.

"Hello, Abe"

"Hello. May I have this dance?"

"Well, uh, I really don't, uhmm," I stood there stammering, unable to form a complete sentence.

"Princess," Beth shouted, saving me from continuing to stammer on like a fool. "We're so happy you came." She hugged me. Apparently she still hadn't accepted I wasn't a hugger. Abe gave me a wink and sly smile.

"Excuse me," he said. "I better check on Ava. Raincheck Karma?"

I nodded. Beth waited for him to leave before she spoke. Her arm rested around my shoulder.

"Listen, Abe told us what happened," she spoke softly so no one could hear. "Oh, he tried to give us some sad drivel about you being sick with flu. But our bullshit radar is always on. We finally got him to tell us the truth. Why didn't you tell us you've been sacked?"

I avoided her gaze. "I figured if Eli found out I no longer had a job and couldn't make rent, he would be forced to ask me to move out. There aren't many flats available in my budget, especially when that budget is zero."

Beth gently grabbed my chin and turned my face hers. She searched my eyes.

"Bullshit."

I shut my eyes tightly to keep the tears that formed from falling. Beth was right.

"You were hurt and betrayed. You were angry and wanted to be left alone. That's okay. We would've understood."

I couldn't stop the tears that slowly fell from my closed eyes.

"But, Princess, know this," Beth spoke with a tough and demanding tone, "we won't allow you to wallow in self-pity. And, for bloody damn sure, we will never allow you to even think about harming yourself. Is that clear?"

I opened my eyes and nodded. My tears stung. Truth be told, it wasn't my tears that stung. It was Beth's all-knowing glare and her words that stung. I believed her. I believed she, Lynn and Eli wouldn't hurt me, nor would they allow anyone else, including me, to do so.

***

The celebration continued on into the night. Everyone danced and laughed as midnight approached. A few of the residents from the neighboring buildings had joined the party. Although I made polite conversation, I mostly sat in the corner and watched everyone have a good time.

Actually, the only time I remembered vacating the corner was when Lynn cut the six-layered chocolate crunch cake.

The cake's appearance hadn't done it justice. The moment I placed a mere morsel in my mouth, the silky-smooth texture brought forth nothing but pure ecstasy. It was a perfect mix of buttery sweetness with just a hint of salty goodness.

The cake was a nod to old-fashioned baking, nothing but real and fresh ingredients and a heavy dose of love mixed in. This cake was a pure culinary luxury. Every bite was heaven on earth.

I wasn't the only one to experience the chocolaty magic carpet ride. By the number of cake crumbs, smears of icing and empty plates, it was clear the cake had lived up to its status as the main attraction.

As midnight approached, the party room quickly emptied and partygoers headed to the roof to watch fireworks and toast in the New Year. I stayed behind to clean. I was sweeping up some glitter and streamers when Abe walked in.

He had taken Ava home and put her to bed. Two slices of Lynn's cake, as well as staying up four hours past her bedtime had taken its toll. Ava had conked out in one of the lounge chairs.

"Why are you in here and not outside watching the fireworks," Abe asked.

"Not a big fan of fireworks. In fact I was just about to head home." I set the broom down and headed toward the exit. Abe grabbed me by the arm and spun me into his chest.

"I'm cashing in my raincheck," he said. I stared dumbfounded at him. "Our dance, remember?"

"I'm ... I'm not much of a dancer and, and there's no music" I babbled.

"That's okay," Abe replied. He pulled me closer and we swayed to the tune he hummed. Outside, the shouts began as the countdown to midnight reached the final ten seconds.

10, 9, 8, 7, 6 —

Abe stopped dancing and just held me.

5, 4, 3 —

He leaned in a little closer and our foreheads touched. His hand rested below my ear and his thumb stroked my cheek. He pulled me even closer until there was no space left between us. I felt his rapidly beating heart against my chest. Or was that my heart?

2 —

He kissed me and obliterated every thought in my never-silent head. Nothing mattered but this moment. His kiss was slow and soft, and it comforted me in ways I never thought possible. My heart fluttered inside and my legs turned to jelly.

1 —

Happy New Year!

Abe rested his forehead against mine when we finally came up for air.

"Happy New Year — Princess," Abe whispered.

CHAPTER 14
THANK YOU

We sat so enthralled in each other we hadn't noticed that the popcorn hadn't made it to our mouths in quite some time.

"Hey will you two stop snogging? You're embarrassing me."

"Sorry, Ava," I said with a smile. Abe chuckled. Ava scoffed and hustled back to her seat. The movie theatre auditorium buzzed with excitement in anticipation for the latest blockbuster to start. The lights dimmed and the picture began to roll. Abe placed his arm around me and gave me a soft kiss, a distraction while he stole some of my popcorn. My heart melted like butter at the sight of him. Our relationship was now entering its sixth month, which was a miracle when I thought about our first date.

That date hadn't gone well. In fact, it began bloody awful and ended horrendously. Abe tried to make conversation but I sat there in awkward silence looking dismayed and disinterested. I wasn't sure how to act or what to say. I also keep spilling things or tripping over something. When I got up to go to the toilet, I bumped into a waiter carrying deserts for the table next to us. The lady seated at the table didn't seem like she enjoyed being covered in strawberries and whipped cream.

It was my very first date ever, unless that mandatory school trip to the cinema where I sat next to a boy I had a crush on counted.

Like normal people, I'd signed up for some of those online dating services a few times before. It didn't take very long to learn the phrase *'it's not you, it's me,'* wasn't just a line actors said on the telly. If it sucked being told this face-to-face, imagine how it felt to be told this over the faceless Internet.

Heck, even desperate men looking for lonely women on *www.needtogetmarriedtostayinthecountry.co.uk* had turned me down.

Our second attempt was a repeat of our first. When Abe walked me to my flat, he gently kissed me on the cheek and said goodbye. I knew there wouldn't be a third date.

"Well that's it. You blew it!" Arrogance returned before my first date with Abe, delivering more witty insults. *"There went your one decent chance at snagging a man. I think it's time to get a cat."*

Arrogance hadn't counted on the Sisters and Eli being my corner men. They arranged what amounted to 'play dates' where Eli pretended to be my date. They each gave me tips on how to act or what to say in different social settings.

Eli also had a man-to-man talk with Abe. Whatever Eli said worked. He'd convinced Abe to take one more shot. The third date went better. It wasn't great, but it wasn't as horrendous as our first.

By our fifth date, I was a little more comfortable, though still a bit awkward. Abe rolled with it and we had slowly worked our way up from strangers to boyfriend and girlfriend.

I learned later that Eli and the Sisters placed bets on how many dates Abe and I would have before we'd end up in bed together.

Lynn won — Lucky #7.

***

I still hadn't found a full-time job yet in the past six months. However, I worked out a compromised with the Sisters and Eli.

What I didn't know when I moved in was that the Sisters and Eli had their fingers in many different pies — construction, grocery sales, toys and some tourist attractions, just to name a few. They even owned several cinemas throughout the country, including the one Abe, Ava and I currently sat in.

They offered me room and board to do the bookkeeping and develop plans to increase their customer base and profits. So far things had gone smoothly.

After the movie, Ava had headed back to her friend's house for the slumber party portion of their evening. Although Abe wasn't always keen, he encouraged Ava to socialize with people her age. My life tales and experiences convinced Abe that Ava's exceptionally high IQ and above-average schoolwork wouldn't necessarily give her those social skills and the friendships that would help her later in life. He took my advice and encouraged Ava to socialize more.

He had even given her and her friends a tour of the police station, though from his perspective, it was more his way of saying *"you hurt my daughter — I'll toss your butt in prison."*

Abe and I entered through the front entrance of our building. We saw Lynn and Beth downstairs. They were dressed to the nines and ready to party the night away.

"Abe, Princess," Beth called out when she saw us. "I don't believe you've met my son Michael. Michael, this is Abe and Karma. Karma is the lady we've told you about, the one who's doing all those wonderful things for our various *projects*."

A man dressed in a tux stepped out from behind Beth and shook Abe's hand.

"Nice to meet you," Abe said. The man turned to shake my hand.

When our eyes met — we both stood there in shock.

"You!" the man gasped. I couldn't believe it. Michael was the man I'd saved from being splattered by the Mercedes.

"Hello, Michael," I shook his hand gently. "Very nice to meet you." Michael stood there. Beth gave him a sharp smack on the back.

"Sorry. Nice to meet you, Karma." We all stood in silence.

"Okay, what the hell is up with you two," Beth asked. She really was a bullshit radar. "You two shag each other or something."

"No!" Michael and I shouted at the same time.

"Then what gives?" Lynn asked.

"C'mon, spit it out," Beth demanded.

"Well, mother," Michael began. "Remember when I told you how I'd almost gotten splattered by a Mercedes—"

"Because your head was looking down at that bloody mobile

125

like always," Beth interrupted. Michael rolled his eyes. Only Abe and I caught it.

"Yes. Well Karma was the lady who prevented that scenario from happening."

The Sisters screeched so loud I thought the mirrors in the lobby would crack. Beth grabbed me in a giant bear hug. The way she nearly squeezed the life out of me didn't exactly erase my fear of huggers.

Abe covered his mouth and tried not to laugh at my silent pleas for help. Beth finally released me, and I sucked in as much oxygen as possible to get my blood flowing again.

"Princess, I can't think of anything to say but thank you. When Michael told us what happened, I thanked the powers that be for that anonymous stranger," Beth said.

"Then she thumped him when Michael said he'd blamed the person for the loss of his mobile and shoes. She thumped even harder when he said he hadn't thanked the person."

"Yes, she did," Michael said. He gently rubbed his head as if the thump happened a few seconds ago and not months. "They've also told me you're bloody good at numbers and research. My company is in need of a new manager for our Analytics department. If you interested I'd like to get together and chat about the job."

"Sure." I said.

"Great. Here's my card. I'll let my assistant know to expect your call and we'll get something scheduled." He handed me his card. "Now, ladies, we must get going if we're to make our reservation."

"Michael's taking us out to celebrate. His company, Insights, just signed a client to the sweet tune of £200 million," Beth said. She beamed at her son while she straightened his bow tie.

"He's gonna make Torrance Clothiers the biggest clothing retailer in the world." They said their goodbyes and headed out to the limo Michael hired.

Abe and I said our goodbyes then we headed to my flat.

***

Abe grabbed me by the waist the moment I closed the door.

He pulled me into him.

"Well, now, Ms. Bailey, I would say things are looking up for you." He kissed me, softly at first, but soon deepened the kiss. When we pulled apart, he ran his hand softly down my cheek. One touch from this man and it was over. My body went weak and I couldn't think about anything other than him and the pleasure he brought to my life.

His left hand dropped to my thigh and pulled up my skirt. I couldn't move even if I tried. And I didn't try. His fingers danced all over me causing a short circuit to my brain.

He turned me around and we spilled onto the couch. Abe's eyes searched mine. I smile and kissed him. My lips felt his mouth open just bit wider, and I slipped him some tongue. He fought the urge to grin and kept kissing me. My mouth pulled away, and he whimpered. I smiled and got to my feet. I pulled him to his feet and we made our way to my bedroom.

In the room Abe stood so close I could breathe in his musky scent. It drove me wild and he knew it. With a laugh, he lifted me off my feet and tossed me onto the bed. Lust, love, passion, heat — we had it all. Abe kissed me breathless.

Then he got down to business.

He pulled off my skirt. I yanked down his pants. His hands moved slowly up my legs, my thighs, my stomach, until they came to rest on my breasts. My hands moved slowly down from his chest and grabbed his manhood. He let out a soft growl and pushed me flat on my back. He covered my body with his and slowly entered my secret palace.

Our tongues locked in a passionate kiss as he thrust slowly. I moaned. He lowered his head and kisses my breasts. His fingers teased my clit.

He thrust again and I moaned. I was on the brink and needed to be taken over the edge.

"Please," I begged. I felt his smile against my cheek.

"As you command, your highness."

Seconds later, he plunged into me harder, deeper, faster, until we both hit our peak and collapsed breathless. I kissed him softly and whispered in his ear.

"Thank you."

CHAPTER 15
REALITY WILL BLOW YOU AWAY

I flicked through the pages of the latest trendy magazine until I found what I searched for — a full-page, color ad for Torrance Clothiers. I smiled.

I'd been at Insights for four months now and things were going well. I still preferred to work alone most of the time, but I had come to enjoy my co-workers' friendly banter. The environment was the complete opposite of the toxic one I experienced at Vixen.

As I skimmed the pages of the magazine, a short article caught my attention. It was a profile of Jessica Paterson, founder and former CEO of Vixen. The article detailed her successes, what led to her resignation and what she was doing now. I felt sad for Jessica, until I read she received a multi-million pound package when she *resigned* as CEO and now lived in a spacious villa in Italy.

There was also a side-piece on how Vixen was trying to rebuild itself under new leadership after the Stephen Charles Quinn scandal. I knew most of this already. Both Tyson and Julia told me some time ago. They had helped me with some projects when I was working for the Sisters and Eli.

Even all this time later, I still had questions about that whole incident. Why had Monica and her boss sabotaged the presentation? Surely they both would receive large bonuses and promotions if Vixen had landed that account. It didn't make sense

128

then and still didn't make sense, now.

Oh, well. I'd been told that I needed to let bygones be bygones, especially after I learned that Monica was now the senior client services manager at Carter Marketing and Public Relations.

I sat in the café and waited for Abe to join me for a quick lunch. Our jobs kept us both busy these last two weeks and we'd hardly seen each other. The tiny café was located midway between his cop station and my office.

The café's exterior wasn't much to write home about, but the inside was warm and jolly with bright lights and colorful walls. The place wasn't crowded, but it had more than a few customers. I ordered a buttery croissant and coffee while I waited for Abe's arrival.

I sipped my coffee and gagged. The coffee was bitter and needed more French vanilla creamer. I headed over to the condiments counter and poured some into my coffee.

"I'll be damned! If it ain't Ms. *Stank-Kay*." The hair on my neck stood up. I recognized the voice. I turned and came face-to-face with Tasha. She and Monica had just entered the café.

"I can't believe they let you out of the insane asylum," Tasha cackled.

"Insane asylum? I thought she was locked up at the zoo?" Monica taunted. "That would explain the smell."

"Will you please slap the snot out of both of them? C'mon, just once — do it, PLEASE," Arrogance urged me. He'd been on vacation these past four months. It looked like the vacation was over.

Monica and Tasha laughed and continued teasing me. I gripped the coffee mug hard but remained silent.

"Glad to see your sense of style has improved a bit. Still, doesn't matter how cute of a sweater you put a dog in, it's still a dog," Monica quipped.

Tasha pretended to brush something from my sweater. "Ugh, what is that?" she said as she shook some imaginary pest from her hand. "Think you need to get a stronger flea collar, *Stank-Kay*."

They cackled at their jokes. Tears began to form in my eyes as I stood there and took their verbal barbs.

"What the heck is wrong with you? Smack the taste out of these tarts' mouths," Arrogance encouraged. *"Oh, my goodness, are you about to cry?*

What the heck? You got a man, a good job, good friends and an awesome flat. Why are you letting these slags get to you? Dang, you're still pathetic."

The barista called Tasha's name and she went to get their drinks.

"Heard you got a job with Insights," Monica said. "Wonder what they'll say if they receive an anonymous call explaining why your previous employer fired you." She chuckled and leaned in closer so only I could hear her.

"I know you know it was me who inserted that video into the presentation. And I bet it's been killing you not knowing why I did it. Why else? Money, of course. Carter PR paid me a huge amount and promised me a senior-level position to sabotage the presentation. Plus, I was still angry with Jessica for choosing that poof Peter over me to be her executive assistant. This way, I finally got my well-deserved promotion, and I got my revenge on both Jessica and Peter."

Monica laughed. I stood in utter disbelief.

"As for you, well you were already considered a big liability to the company. That made it easier to pin the blame on you. I knew no one would believe you over me."

Every word from her mouth stung. My fists clenched and my jaw ached. A hot, burning rage screamed throughout my body, demanding a violent release.

"Hit her! Hit her! Hit her! She's the reason you went through hell. She's the reason the boy killed himself, and why you almost done yourself in. Please, punch her lights out."

"No, don't. She is not worth it. Not one wee bit."

I remained composed. Arrogance pushed for me to lose control and punch Monica, but Common Sense advised me to resist.

I chose Common Sense over Arrogance.

"How did you get the video and fake the IT logs?" I calmly asked.

"Oh, I didn't fake the logs. I conned Vince to do it. Funny what a man would do when he thinks he's gonna sample the honey pot. Now, getting the video? That was a little harder. That dumbass cop, Jaikan, was that his name? Doesn't matter, I've had so many I can't keep track. Anyway, I learned he did private security work for some rich poofs and he stumbled across the video. The wanker wouldn't give it up until I gave him a little sample of my *sweetness*. Longest two minutes of my life."

I gagged.

"You know, I felt a little sad when I heard he died. Then again he shouldn't have stolen my last tin of tobacco that morning. As for Vince? Well, when the fallout from the scandal heated up, I emailed an anonymous tip that someone tampered with the company's servers. Vixen hired a private IT team to investigate and they found he'd tampered with some other files, too. He was fired him about two months after they tossed your smelly arse out."

She laughed then walked over to Tasha and grabbed her coffee. I stood dumbfound. It had been Monica's tobacco that killed Jaikan. I remembered the look on his face before he dropped to the floor. He must have realized it before his head smacked that concrete floor.

I was so awestruck by what Monica had told me, I didn't even realize Abe had arrived until he tapped my shoulder.

"Hey, beautifu—" He saw my face. "What's wrong? What happened?"

On the verge of tears, I said, "Nothing. Let's go somewhere else. They aren't serving the split pea soup today." I grabbed my purse from the table and headed to the exit. Abe, confused, followed me. He caught up and gently grabbed me by the arm.

"Hey, hey. Slow down. Good. Now, tell me what's up?"

"Nothing. It's nothing. I just wanted split pea soup today, that's all."

"You hate split pea soup. Now, tell me what's wrong."

The door swung opened before I responded. A man dressed in a button-down dress shirt and dress slacks rushed in.

"Monica, you bitch," he roared. The man's outburst surprised everyone. No one moved or said a word. All eyes were on the man and Monica.

"Richie, *Sweetie!* What are you on about?" Monica whimpered like a teenager.

"What am I on about?" the man shook his head in disbelief. "You know what I'm on about, you vicious little whore. You set me up, you slag. Then you sent the video to my wife?"

Monica laughed. She truly was an idiot without a care for anyone but herself.

"She's divorcing me and now she won't let me see my children," Richie cried.

"I would say *sorry*," she huffed, "but I feel it's my duty to let wives know when their husbands can't keep their willies in their pants. Oh, and thanks for the new Mercedes and the diamond bracelet."

Monica and Tasha laughed. Everyone in the café stared in total disbelief at the two women's attitudes.

Fury and hatred smoldered in Richie eyes. Revenge on his mind. Both Abe and I knew it. What we didn't know was how Richie would enact his revenge.

But we didn't have to wait long to find out.

The gunshot cracked the air louder than thunder. The bullet blew Monica's head wide open and painted the wall with blood and brain matter.

Richie lowered the gun. His hand and arm shook at his side as the realization of what he had just done took hold of him. The adrenaline that had coursed through his veins just moments ago was beginning to fade. His body was shutting down, along with his ability to think logically. He wanted to run away, but he couldn't; his legs wouldn't move.

He turned and saw the shocked and terrified faces. For the moment, he just stood there. Then he started to cry. He pointed the gun at Tasha and cocked.

Abe moved quicker than lightning and pinned Richie to the wall. They struggled over the weapon. Abe slammed Richie's gun hand twice again the wall hard, forcing Richie to drop the firearm.

Abe punched Richie in the stomach. Richie gasped at the pain but he remained determined.

He punched Abe in the jaw. The punch momentarily stunned Abe, which allowed Richie to grab the gun again. Abe grabbed at the pistol and they struggled for what seemed like forever.

Bang!

The two men stared at each other for a moment. Then Abe fell backwards onto the floor. His hands clutched his side. Richie stood there in a stupefied haze. A few other men in the café tackled Richie and held him down. Someone kicked the gun out of the Richie's reach.

I don't remember if I screamed but I guess I did. I rushed over to Abe and held him. Blood gushed out in a constant flow. My fingers closed over the wound but Abe's blood poured out through his fingers and mine.

"Stay with me. Help is on the way. Please stay with me," I cried. "Please."

Abe tried to speak but no words came. His pulse grew weaker with each muffled breath.

"Save your strength. Don't say anything." Tears flowed from my eyes.

Abe's bloodied fingers gently grasped mine. He squeezed tightly as he stared up at me. He smiled.

It was the same smile he gave me the first time we met; the same smile he gave at the New Year's Eve party; the same smile he gave after our first kiss.

It was the same smile he gave me this morning when I woke up in his arms. It was the smile I wanted to wake up to for the rest of my life.

That smile soon faded.

And so did Abe.

"You were right. You won't ever have a 'happily ever after,' will you?" Arrogance softly reminded me.

CHAPTER 16
LIFE GOES ON

Two years later

"Sara? Did we get the analytics workup for Ames Financial?" I asked my executive assistant.

"Yes, ma'am," Sara answered. "Tyson hand-carried it up here himself this morning. He said Julia took the day off to attend her son's football game. Did you know they're playing for the championship?"

I smiled. "Yes I knew. If they win, Julia said she would buy coffee and pastries for everyone in the department."

I'd convinced Michael to hire Tyson and Julia. Together we revitalized Insight's analytics department and helped the company snag many lucrative accounts.

They both, along with Mr. Russell, had been sacked from Vixen Marketing about three months after me. I had made Mr. Russell a lucrative offer to join us at Insights, but he said retirement was best for him. He now lived in a small French country village and spent his days fishing and mastering the art of French cooking.

A year after the Quinn scandal, Vixen Marketing entered insolvency and had eventually been completely liquidated about ten months ago. Most of the employees found jobs with other firms. A few even worked at Insights, though I'm happy to say none were in my department.

Sara returned her attention to her computer. She was extremely efficient and always dressed to the nines. Her glossy shoes to her pearl necklace made her look much older than her youthful age of twenty-six. Her suit was tailored and her shirt ironed flawlessly.

Although British by birth, her accent had been mangled during her six years abroad in the States. Sara was also a big hit with the Sisters. Whenever they stopped by for a visit, the three dissolved into passionate discussions about the latest Hollywood hunk, diva or latest blockbusters. Sara also provided the Sisters with the latest fashion tips for seniors.

Every now and then I caught Sara doing some online shopping instead of work. Since the shops were clients of Insights, I allowed it under the guise of market research, so long as it didn't affect her daily tasks.

"Sara, have we received the contracts from legal? They said they'd have them ready before lunch."

"No, ma'am," Sara replied. "I'll call down and see what's the hold up."

"Would it be too much to ask if you could go down there in person?"

Sara had a way with people I never possessed. She was able to talk people into dropping what they were doing and fulfill her requests.

"No, ma'am. Not at all."

"Thank you."

Sara locked her computer and pinned her security access badge to her blouse.

"Plus, I bet Paul would love to see you? When you're done at legal, take an extended lunch."

Her smile was wider than the Grand Canyon. "Thanks boss." She grabbed her purse and hightailed out the office.

I watched her go then leaned back in my chair and stared at the photo on the corner of my desk. It was a photo of Abe, Ava and me taken during one of Ava's school holidays.

I stared at the photo and wondered what my life could've been. Abe's and my relationship hadn't been easy. My issues got the better of me at times and led me to distance myself from him.

After his chat with Eli, Abe didn't let me push him completely away. It took me a long time to realize the man was my angel, my soulmate. He was the one person who could keep me sane in a world full of chaos, whether the chaos was real or just a figment of my over-active imagination.

Most amazingly, Abe had an uncanny sense of timing. He had known when to let me have my moments and exactly when to pull me out of my misery. He had listened to my problems and I had listened to his. We had both known the road ahead would be rocky, but we accepted the challenge.

Now, every time I thought of him — those beautiful blue eyes, his delicious bum and that wicked grin — I couldn't help but smile.

"I see your assistant is off to take care of another of her highness's errands," came a voice from the office door. I looked up and beamed.

Speak of my angel.

Abe leaned against my office door, exuding delicious sexiness. He'd recently been promoted to detective sergeant. My handsome man looked darn good in his dark Hugo Boss business suit. He stepped in and closed the door.

Every time I saw him, I remembered the first time he kissed me with those beautiful, round, sultry, succulent lips. The kiss was soft and sweet, and it turned me inside-out.

There are still times when my overactive brain brought up memories of that frightening day in the café. My body shuddered every time I remembered how I almost lost Abe. Then he would kiss me and I forgot the craziness for a while.

"Hi, love. How's your day been?" I asked. "I'm sorry I left so early this morning. I had a few reports to get done. How can I make it up to you?"

"Lunch will do," he replied.

"Sure. There's this great Greek place around the corner that everyone has been —?"

My breath caught as Abe kissed me and gently pushed me back into my chair. Why was it all he had to do was kiss me, and I handed over the keys to the kingdom?

"Because you're such a sad sap who needs —"

Oh, shut the hell up Arrogance!

"Hmmm," I moaned. His lips gracefully trailed their way to my left hand. He smiled at the exquisite diamond ring he'd placed on my finger exactly fifteen months ago. He kissed my hand softly and helped me to my feet, before leaning me against the edge of my desk.

Abe's hand snaked its way up my blouse and squeezed my right tit. I smiled. He always went to the right. He grinned and playfully smacked my hand away when I tried to remove his.

"Detective Sergeant, I must say this is highly inappropriate behavior," I began. "What if someone walked in?" His hypnotizing blue eyes stared deep into mine with a promise of more sexy delightfulness. He gave me that sexy smile as he slowly unbuttoned my blouse.

"Mrs. Eason let's review a few facts. One — you just gave your assistant an extended lunch. Two — I know your next meeting isn't until two o'clock. And three —" he nibbled on my ear. "No one who valued their life would dare to walk into your office without knocking?"

He slowly lifted me onto my desk and gently pressed his hard manhood against me. I moaned. His lips brushed my ear as he asked, "have I told you how much I love you?"

"Yes. But actions speak louder than words," I teased and hoped he would soon extinguish the fire burning inside me.

My back arch in anticipation as I watch him slowly, and provocatively, unzipped his pants. I softly growled as his rod teased my secret folds.

Abe leaned over and pushed me flat onto the desk. He whispered my name over and over while he passionately took me to heaven.

Lunchtime on payday Friday wasn't a dreadful experience anymore.

EPILOGUE
IT'S RAINING MEN

The rain fell steadily throughout the night but had ceased by the time I woke up. Sunshine slowly broke through the remaining clouds.

Abe had been called to a crime scene before daybreak, so it was just Ava and I. We spent the day talking, shopping and having lunch at, according to Ava, the "trendiest and coolest" restaurant ever. Afterwards, we'd visited a few museums.

Ava was at a sleepover at a friend's later that evening, so I relaxed on the couch.

Well, relaxed in my own unique way, reassessing a new Insights client's financial summary.

It was after seven in the evening when Abe came home. He was in a state of utter amusement. He gave me a quick peck on the cheek and hung up his coat.

"Let us in on the joke?" I asked.

"Well, you're not gonna believe this but the call I got this morning? It was in response to a man who'd been pushed out of the window of his third-floor hotel room by his wife."

Abe laughed so hard he cried. I was flabbergasted at his reaction. Abe wasn't a spiteful person so his current demeanor baffled me.

"Oh, my goodness. I don't think that is funny," I admonished.

Abe regained his composure, somewhat.

"Wait until you've heard the whole tale."

He proceeded to tell me that the wife had learned the husband was having an affair and followed him to the hotel. She convinced the maid that she'd lock herself out of the room. When the maid opened the door, the wife barged in and caught her husband — in flagrante delicto — with another man.

My jaw dropped.

"Is that when she pushed him out the window?" I asked.

"No. According to the maid, the wife laughed, called the husband all kinds of nasty names and said she couldn't wait to negotiate her divorce settlement. The wife was about to leave when the other man called her a fat hippo who couldn't get a man hot if she lit him on fire."

I sat up straight in anticipation of what happened next.

"The wife tackled the other man and pummeled him. The husband managed to pull them apart just as hotel security arrived. Security was escorting the wife out the room when the husband dropped another bombshell."

I was totally invested in this story by now and teetered on every word.

"The husband then told the wife he had been born a woman. He had sex reassignment surgery two years before they met. And that's when the wife snapped. She charged at the husband and pushed him out the window."

"Oh, my goodness. He's not—"

"No, he's not dead. He hit the hotel's awning and rolled off. He broke quite a few bones and has a concussion, but doctors said he'll be okay." Abe chuckled.

"This was a very serious incident. I don't see what's so hysterical," I scolded. Abe gave me a kiss then sat next to me on the couch.

"What if I were to tell you that the wife was one Mary St. Charles. I believe she was an acquaintance of yours?"

I sat speechless. Mary.

The same Mary St. Charles who had at one time wished I become the latest guest of Her Majesty's Prison systems. Now, not only would that soon be her fate, but she'd been humiliated in the process.

I tried to hold in the laughter, but I couldn't. I laughed and laughed all night long.

Fate, or should I say Karma, always gets the last laugh.

FROM THE AUTHOR

Thank you for reading *My Name is Karma.*

I hope you enjoyed this story.

When I'm not working my daily nine-to-five job, I spend most of my time exploring my imagination, documenting the wacky adventures of the various characters that spring to life.

More of my tales can be found online at *candyknightstories.wordpress.com*

Made in the USA
Lexington, KY
22 March 2018